A HISTORY OF EXISTING LIFE

A History of Existing Life

And Other Stories

Shelagh Powers Johnson

BROKEN TRIBE PRESS

CONTENTS

For Jack,

forever part of the story

AND YET

A baby has arrived in the main house, and unrest now hangs in the air like wet summer heat. The girl can hear his wails sifting through the trees, shuddering and mournful—this dark child so intent on misery, born with some terrible knowledge of the future lodged in his bones.

She is sitting on her cot, knees folded to her chest; the child's father is in her cabin again, and he has wedged the cot into the space between the door and table to keep others from coming inside. He reaches for her and she shrinks back, a learned lessening, but he barely touches her as he presses a halved walnut into the cup of her hand. She stares down at his offering, weighing this act of kindness in her open palm, then digs at the nut nestled inside, the flat open wings of it loosening and dislodging between her fingers. She lifts it to her lips and the wet meat is sweet on her tongue. He lifts her chin with his finger so that she is looking up at him, and his eyes are dark and mirthless.

She knows, of course, what this will cost her. Her body knows the math of it, understands the taking of one thing for the relinquishment of another. He pulls a second walnut from his pocket and cracks it open like a memory: his hands snapping the necks of hares, of chickens; the snap of a whip in his hand as it comes down hard and fast. He shakes the nut loose from its shell and slips it between her parted lips, then lowers himself down beside her.

She lies back, searching for the splintered seam above her where the wall meets the roof. She finds her favorite spot, the whorl of knotted wood that curls and twists like what she imagines the body of a hurricane might look like, what her own heart might look like: the tight red fist of it kneading inside her, stubborn to the forces that have tried to still it. She imagines that it is her actual heart nested in the wood above her, a dark burl that can beat outside her body until it's safe to return. This soothes her against the urgent rock of him: his collection of her bottomless debt.

He's gentle this afternoon, the drink on his breath a balm rather than a poison, and when he falls asleep, his breathing is steady and calm. His peacefulness is a wonder to her when she witnesses it; Monsieur Aubigny is himself a hurricane, a knot of anger unspooling into brutality, and she is grateful for the slim mercy of a few tender hours.

In the dim light of the cabin his skin is the color of sun-baked clay—dark against her own, which is fair as buttercream and dotted with freckles—and she's reminded of the lore that hangs heavy here like its own circling hurricane. But the mythology of L'Abri has not weakened over time like the will of a storm, instead gathering strength as new questions form about this strange, foreign master, as truths bend with the years and a whispered oral history continues taking shape.

The arrival of the Aubigny baby in the main house had felt to her like a held breath, weeks suspended in waiting as the newborn plumped into a milk-fat infant, his puckered skin smoothing, his features crystallizing. The mother, Aubigny's young wife, was silly with love, in awe of this little creature in the blind way of new mothers, but the other inhabitants of L'Abri searched the child's face for a legend to help them decipher the past and prophesy the future. They stole glances when his nursemaid walked him around the garden in her arms, pointing out the waxy pink buds on spring trees and the push of crocuses at her feet. The grounds of L'Abri exploded with color in the springtime, an eerie contrast to the main house, which was meticulously maintained and yet somehow wholly inhospitable. The estate was surrounded by indigo fields, neat blue rows shouldering the bayou that lurked on the edge of Aubigny's land, a patchwork of beauty and peril. The nurse murmured to the child as she walked, whispering to him the names of flowers: *d'échinacée, des tulipes, d'asclépiade.* The child peered up at her from the folds of blanket with a ferocious intensity, his face a creamy brown against the pale muslin, a dark stigma emerging from a wreath of clean white petals.

Aubigny stirs beside the girl and she stiffens. She feels him push closer to her, his breath hot on her neck. "La Blanche," he murmurs into her hair, his voice hoarse from sleep. His fingers graze her bare stomach, trace the sharp rise of her hip bones. And then: "The white one."

He has said this to her before—the meaning of her name in English, chosen for her by the woman who delivered her here in this cabin the night her mother fainted from the strain of childbirth and never awoke.

The girl had been born so pale she was nearly blue, her skin translucent and her body sapped of oxygen by the cord wrapped tight around her throat. Sometimes she wonders if perhaps her mother would have lived if she herself had died that night; if perhaps there is a simple and just equation to survival, a finite well of humanity, and her mother had simply tipped her own life into La Blanche's cup. A first and last act of devotion.

Aubigny ladders his fingers up the pale stretch of her inner arm. La Blanche's skin had darkened only slightly over the years, the papery white of it a story told to her in fragments and variations: her father had likely been a friend of the Aubignys, visiting from a nearby plantation; or perhaps he'd come to L'Abri on business and taken a liking to the pretty young girl working in the main house; maybe he had been a distant relative, staying at L'Abri after the death of his wife, after the blight of his crops, after the destruction of his estate in a fire, in a hurricane, in an uprising. Stories flowed here like the wild weave of a river.

"The white one," Aubigny whispers again, slowly, as if to savor the sound of it. And then in his native French: "C'est vrai. Très blanche." His fingers pause at the base of her neck where her hair is damp with sweat. His smile is menacing, joyless. "Et pourtant." *And yet.*

He wraps a curl of her hair around his finger and she feels a buried memory rise to the surface, unbidden: her hair held in his closed fist; the crack of bones as his boot kicks at her face, at the telling swell of her abdomen; her body dragged limp and broken back to the steps of her cabin in the middle of the night. He first began coming for her when she was barely twelve, and she has pushed four lives into the world since then. Her children were born a breathing currency, owed as soon as her sons' limbs had shed their childish softness and her daughters' hands had learned the tidy rhythm of women's work. Twice La Blanche caught herself in time, recognized the roiling nausea and the firm round of her belly before it was too late; her sister Josèphine knows Louisiana's roots and herbs, understands the precious alchemies that make things happen, that make things not happen. In a few years, La Blanche's girls will be netted by the phases of the moon and her own place at L'Abri will shift: her body will learn new uses as their young bodies learn to disappear under the weight of force, as their hearts travel to safe hidden spaces outside of themselves. Sometimes the impossible truth of this burns so hot in her gut that her only salve is the thought of her sister's hands: snipping leaves from angry red plants, unearthing leathery mushrooms from soil, crumbling these deadly treasures into a stone mortar. La Blanche pictures a blanket of powder dusted over Aubigny's dinner or into his glass of whiskey. She imagines herself sprinkling poisons into his open, sleeping mouth, and the lump of furious sorrow softens enough for her to go on living.

La Blanche had not lost the baby the night Aubigny attacked her, though there had been a moment when she'd been certain both she and her unborn child would not survive his drunken fury. L'Abri had seen disappearances before, women perhaps sold off but likely swallowed by the bayou after committing invisible sins against him. These women were swept into the lore of the place, woven into the story of how the plantation had come to be this way: purchased by a kind, older master who named the estate—L'Abri, *the shelter*—and who demanded nothing but a calm and genial order; the man's mysterious Parisian wife who was never seen but around whom a branch of story grew; the confounding portrait of a beautiful, brown-skinned woman, hung in the library and then quickly removed; and finally the couple's dark, troubled son—this younger Aubigny—arriving from France after his mother's death in Paris, tyranny coursing like blood through his veins.

The girl can hear the faraway cries of the new baby in the main house, low and plaintive at first and then rising to a piercing crescendo. Aubigny curses under his breath, a flicker of rage sparking, settling, and then he rises from the cot and pulls his pants from around his ankles, snapping his suspenders up over his broad shoulders. She pictures the child's nurse blowing cool air onto the baby's round cheeks, tickling the pads of his feet with her fingertips, buttoning and unbuttoning his layette to warm him up, to cool him down.

She notices Aubigny watching her and his expression is grim and unreadable. Without warning, he reaches down and grabs one of her breasts, his ragged nails digging into her skin to dispel any suggestion of tenderness. She bites down on her lip to keep from crying out, pictures the angry bruise that will soon bloom there. His fingers pinch hungrily at her nipple, but his eyes are lustless. "Nasty woman," he mutters, and then he yanks the cot away from the door so there's space enough for him to pass. "*Putain.*"

And then he's gone. She watches his retreating figure through the cracked door, the dying sunlight silhouetting him until he's nothing but a smudge of black in the distance. This is the way he always leaves her—with some hateful valediction so she never mistakes his taking for giving. So she knows that in this taking he has diminished her, and that the day will come when he will whittle her down to nothing.

*

Weeks later, word spreads that Aubigny's wife and baby have disappeared from L'Abri. The child's nurse is blank with grief and offers no explanations for their departure, only shakes her head and stares down at the empty bowl of her arms, folded to her stomach as if the baby were lifted from them only a moment before. The cook says they've gone to live with the woman's mother; she pinches at the brown skin of her forearm, whispers that Monsieur Aubigny banished them both from the house. "Il ne tolérera pas un enfant comme ça." *He'll not tolerate a child like that.*

But then, a second tale begins to simmer beneath this one: some men in the fields saw the woman holding her baby the day she vanished from L'Abri, saw her standing at the base of the path leading from the plantation back toward her family home. She wore only a thin chemise and her hair hung loose, long and coppery, as if she'd just risen from sleep. These men say they saw the woman turn away from the path and walk into the tall grasses, the baby clutched to her chest. They say they watched her disappear into the copse of trees that led out into the mouth of the bayou but that they didn't dare follow her, the crime of abandoned work met with its own horrors.

For a time, La Blanche still expects the mother and child to reappear in the main house. She knows the tides of Aubigny's moods, knows how the crash of his anger can recede into the gentle pull of something almost like atonement. But as weeks pass without their return, an understanding settles over the plantation that their place here was only ever temporary, their life at L'Abri a failed experiment stricken from its history. La Blanche thinks of what the men in the fields saw, and of the way the slow-churning water beyond the plantation laps at the roots of trees, devours the slender trunks of tupelos and chews away at the thick, ropy bark of cypresses. She cannot fathom the woman walking her baby into such an abyss, and so she allows herself to imagine them back at the woman's family home—away from the bayou and Aubigny—though perhaps some stifled part of her knows they have succumbed to both monsters.

*

It's a cool autumn evening when Aubigny tells the men to build a bonfire behind the main house. La Blanche stands with her daughters on the edge of the clearing and watches her eldest, Mathieu, gathering kindling from beneath the tall oaks. He looks like both a child and a man: his face is round and smooth, his eyes the color of wildflower honey and bright with life, but his body has the hollowed, sinewy contours of someone roughened by time. La Blanche has watched this gradual lessening of men through the years, has seen over and over all the ways this place carves away at them too. Soon, she knows, the light in her child's eyes will begin to dwindle, and the sweet bell of his voice will harden, and this ebbing will be its own kind of death.

The fire starts small, a circle of flames hardly large enough to roast meat on a spit. After a while, Aubigny appears in the back doorway carrying a wide wicker basket piled high with bright, silky fabrics, and La Blanche's other son, her youngest child, is standing behind him. It isn't until Aubigny places the basket in the doorway and walks back into the house that she sees what her son is holding, and her breath catches in her throat as she watches him walk solemnly toward the bonfire. He places the willow cradle into the center of the flames with such earnest ceremony that it's as if the baby is still asleep inside, a sacrifice laid out on the pyre. And then the wicker basket is carried over to the fire as well, and the rest of Aubigny's grisly offerings are set ablaze: the child's tiny white layette, the mother's dresses and petticoats, her evening gloves and hats and the soft linen frocks she'd worn to accommodate the rise of her stomach before the baby was born. La Blanche turns away when she sees Mathieu toss an embroidered quilt onto the pile, remembering how the nursemaid had bundled the child into it right after he was born, walked him proudly around the grounds as if he were her own perfect creation.

La Blanche, relegated to the gardens and the quiet dark of her cabin, had known little of Monsieur Aubigny's life inside the main house. She had recognized the strange dissonance of his marriage—his wife pure and lovely, Aubigny a deep well of cruelty—and had appreciated the woman's wide smile, ever-present for over a year and then simply gone: a candle blown out. She'd known the child's inconsolable cries and accepted them as a kind of wisdom, an understanding of the atrocities he'd been born into. But she had not known this mother and child. She couldn't conjure the sound of the woman's voice in her memory, or recall the exact shade of the baby's eyes. And yet their erasure gnaws at her now, weeks of buried dread rising like bile in her throat. The woman is dead; the child is dead. She understands these truths with a sudden, bitter certainty, just as she understands that her own survival has been owed only to chance. Because the world had tried to choke the life out of her the moment she crowned into it; Aubigny had nearly beaten two lives from her body the night he'd chosen her as his prey; and all the while, the bayou has stirred lazily in the distance, bubbling and hungry, a whispered threat. She knows that she could be wiped clean from this place without ceremony, an offering made to the murky waters without even the glint of a candle flame to announce her end. She understands the precarious mercy of her children waking with the sun each day and surviving past its setting.

By midnight, the bonfire has died out almost completely, fed its final scraps just past dusk and then abandoned. La Blanche had watched it for hours, mirrored in the large bay windows at the back of the house, wild and warped by the panes of glass where Aubigny stood surveying the scene—the refracted firelight a hellish wreath around him, a devil engulfed in flames.

She'd allowed herself to imagine these flames bending with the wind, hot tongues licking at the shutters of the house, crawling across the low-hanging eaves, wrapping outstretched fingers around the thick columns of the terrace. She'd thought of the bookshelves lining the walls of the library, the burnished wood of Aubigny's gleaming dining table, the stacks of firewood placed beside the hearth in the parlor. Kindling poised for an errant spark. A blameless crime of nature.

But this fire had been built expertly, tidily, far enough from the main house that it could thrash and flail without disaster: a beast contained and sated, the scorched remains of all it had devoured now a pile of bones sucked dry. Barely burning coals crackle in the wreckage and La Blanche recognizes the blackened husk of the child's cradle, the braided willow a delicate ribcage with an ember glowing feebly at its center. She thinks of the tight burl of wood in her cabin, her nested heart sheltered in the planks. She pictures the curl and flare of it—perhaps less a hurricane and more a flame.

The ember pulses hot beneath the char, the stubborn beat of a heart in the ruins. She stares down at it, this angry bead of fire, then looks up at the main house, at its wide-open windows, thick curtains billowing in the breeze. Surely something so diminished as a smoldering coal would be too weak to set such a place ablaze. Surely a fire that has been so nearly extinguished has no will left to spread.

And yet.

La Blanche reaches down and scoops up a handful of dirt and ash, red radiating at its center. She walks slowly toward the open window, blows gently on this living thing intent on surviving, watches it breathe in her hands. Marvels at all that it can still do.

JUMP

The story begins like a closed fist, tight and finite. The facts are simple, unchanging. It happened how it happened; no need to wonder. But over time, the fingers begin to uncurl, stretching and searching, as if maybe there is more to know—as if maybe the past is a malleable thing. And then the hand opens, flattens, the palm like an offering: I have a story for you.

No one noticed when he slipped away from the party and up to the hosts' bedroom. He took his shoes off, tucked them in a corner; he left a half-drunk beer on the bedside table as if he might come back for it later. It's hard to say what compelled him to do what he did next: maybe he didn't know the pool had been drained for the winter and the jump was nothing more than a misguided party trick, something to liven things up; maybe from the second story window the tarp thrown over the hollow ground had looked soft and inviting, a cushion to break his fall, to scoop him into its folds and toss him up and away; maybe the darkness below had been a welcome mouth, the beast he'd been seeking to swallow him whole.

A picture of his wife had surfaced on the internet a month before, an artsy shot with the blurred hint of nakedness, the camera focused on her face so you could see the lines that had begun whittling their way around her eyes and mouth. It had seemed like an odd injustice, this mildly erotic picture being so unflattering—maybe he'd felt a sliver of sadness for her tucked somewhere beneath his own anger and hurt. It hadn't been their bed she was on; it hadn't been him behind the camera. Still, maybe he wished she'd looked beautiful. Maybe then the world would have been kinder to them. Maybe then the sidelong glances would have been edged with jealousy rather than pity, rather than with disdain. If she'd been young, her hair a silky gold that didn't glint with silver, her body an invitation rather than an apology—maybe then everything would have been different.

After the jump, there were weeks of quiet. The rumors slowed; the picture stopped flashing across cell phone screens; there were no more snarky captions. Instead, people brought her tuna casseroles and frozen lasagnas, a gift certificate for a maid service, for a massage, for a year of free oil changes. She was cradled in the soft palm of sympathy while whispers about what she had done, about why he had jumped, were stifled within a balled fist, closed but ready to punch. She couldn't be both a widow and a whore, so for a little while she was armored by her grief.

But tragedies turn stale in the open air—they need dark corners and the wet must of secrets, edges that morph in the shadows. People need to have a story to tell, a handful of truth to work between their fingers until the facts bend into new angles. They need to burrow deep into the comfort of other people's mistakes, curl themselves around the dimpled flesh of these imperfections, imagine the jump again and again to remind themselves that they are still whole.

BOUND

In her more brutal moments, Maeve would say that the wrong child had survived: when the whiskey set in just as the soft rise of her daughter's voice hit a particularly feminine note; when the girl undressed in the dark and the candlelight bent in her direction, catching on the hairless opal of her skin.

"Like mulberry silk," Marie says, fingertips tracing the inner stretch of her arm, the paper-thin skin of her wrist. "Like the belly of a baby." She smiles, her teeth crooked as the crags of a cliff, her cheeks rutted with scars. "I think you're beautiful both ways." Her voice is quiet, emptied of its playfulness.

The girl withdraws her arm quickly, knowing as she does that Marie will misread her, that the open moon of this kind woman's face will darken at her cowardliness. She knows that Marie can't understand the impossibility of such tenderness existing in the girl's narrow orbit: *you're beautiful both ways.* The girl has only ever known all parts of herself to be wrong.

A notch below useless, you are, Maeve used to mutter as she wrapped coarse scraps of fabric around her daughter's slight frame, so taut that the girl's breath came in ragged gasps. Her breasts were small then, nascent, but the modest swell of her chest drew attention to the way certain clothes dipped in tellingly at the waist, belled out at the hips. Her hair was chopped short, cut crude and jagged to offset any glimmer of loveliness that might threaten to surface, and her small stature translated to a scrappy boyishness when her clothes hung long and loose. On days she went out on her own, she pulled a cap low over her brow, tufts of shorn hair poking out at odd angles like the fronds of a cabbage palm, her mother's words playing in her head. *Eyes to the ground, child,* the voice would chide. *Is binn béal ina thost.* A gruff idiom carried over from Ireland: *It's a sweet mouth that's quiet.*

The girl had learned early how to make herself small, how to become a mute and slender presence—in public to avoid any close attention, at home to shrink from her mother's rage. Her life was itself small, a tight ambit that contracted as she grew older, as the truth became harder to conceal. The ruse had been effortless in babyhood, simple enough when she was a small child: passersby had smiled at the blue of her eyes, the peach glow of her cheeks and, seeing the way the child was dressed, commented on what a handsome little fellow she was.

Marie drops her hands into her lap but doesn't move away, and her nearness without her touch feels to the girl like an urgent, bated breath. Marie can't be much older than she is—twenty at most—but there's a wholeness to her, an abundance, like she's already a finished thing. "Charity," she says, and the girl feels an ache in her chest at the sound of her name. She has only ever been Charity within the confines of her own house; it's a name Maeve often spat at her like an accusation, as if the girl's existence were itself a charitable act, alms paid begrudgingly and warranting no further goodwill. But in Marie's mouth the word sounds sweet, a kindness rather than a plea.

In the outside world, Charity has always been Charles, named for a dead man—a man who'd gone missing before she was conceived and was found washed up on the river's edge before she was born. Her half-brother had been named for him first but hadn't lived long enough to need any name at all; the girl was born a breathing ghost who arrived soon after the sick boy departed, an illegitimate named for the family she'd intruded upon.

Charity didn't know who her real father was, knew only that the math of her conception presented a snag in the smooth fabric of Maeve's reputation and that his true identity was as irrelevant as her own. She was a bastard born on the heels of a beloved, dead child, and so she'd stepped into that child's life—so that Maeve could collect a monthly allowance from the child's grandmother, so that the shame of Charity's existence could vanish along with her identity.

When the grandmother was still alive, Maeve would dress Charity in suspenders and pressed trousers for their monthly visits, her lips set in a thin line and her fingertips poised to pinch at the slightest misstep. *Not a peep from you,* she'd hiss, once Charity was old enough to understand the words, old enough to grasp the general shape of her mother's deceit. Mercifully, the old woman wanted the child's company in presence only, seemingly of the belief that children should remain wordless, sexless creatures until their words held weight, until their genders were of procreative use. There were a few times when the woman seemed to sense some wrongness in the child—noting the small hands, the narrow shoulders, the utter unease—but her ambivalence eclipsed her suspicions and she'd simply turn away with a tut of disapproval.

*

Charity had met Marie walking to one of the odd jobs she worked now that her brother's inheritance had dwindled to almost nothing. She found work that demanded little interaction and light but meticulous, concentrated labor. She was strong for her size, an attribute cultivated to distract fellow laborers from the delicate line of her jaw, the bow of her lips, the elegant and knotless curve of her throat. By now this public self had crystallized so completely that it felt almost chosen; she'd lived outwardly as a boy for nearly eighteen years, her identity so cleanly bisected that she knew no other way to be. That other people didn't unbind their bodies at the end of each day, shed their outer selves like a second skin, was a fact she rarely considered.

Marie had somehow understood the situation immediately—recognized both halves of Charity, decoded the secret split of her. "Hey, honey," Marie had called out from the porch of the old house that first day, her body draped over the railing and her red hair glinting in the sunlight, breasts pushing up from the laced neckline of her dress. Charity always walked on the opposite side of the street when she had to pass that stretch of road: the women who lived in the house often stood out front, yelling obscenities and grabbing the elbows of passing men, cigarette stubs hanging from their open mouths. She'd heard her mother gossip about these women, about the men in town who were known to accept their advances. Of course, she knew what happened inside this house, understood it in the flimsy way she understood that rain fell from clouds, that invisible forces tethered her to the earth, that bodies birthed bodies. But the facts of the act mystified her, and it seemed impossibly brazen that this house was designed for such a thing. Heavy curtains hung in the windows, stripes of candlelight visible between the gaps like a glimpse into something forbidden—the glow of a hidden world within.

"You," Marie had called out again. "Mister, miss, whoever you are. I'll take you either way." She'd laughed then, a loud, joyful laugh that stirred something in Charity despite the growing dread in her gut at being found out. She walked faster, but the woman persisted. "Ask for Marie if you come see me, beautiful." Another sweet bay of laughter. Charity's temples were slick with sweat and she pressed a hand to her forehead, that last word lodging inside her, pulsing in time with the pound of her footsteps: *beautiful, beautiful, beautiful.*

That afternoon, she'd found herself walking home along Marie's side of the road. The sound of the woman's voice was clear in her mind, the words a wild storm beginning to churn, stirring the still landscape inside her. *Mister, miss, whoever you are.* The revelation stated so simply, benign as a morning greeting.

Charity stopped when she reached the house, allowing herself to stare up at it rather than hurrying past as she always had. The place was large but run-down; the faded green shutters that bracketed the windows hung at odd angles, and there were wide gaps in the porch railing, the missing spindles like pulled teeth.

"You need some company, baby?" a woman out front called to her, and Charity startled at the sound. The woman was older, with silvery brown hair and pale skin etched with lines.

She shook her head. "Is Marie here?" she asked, and then immediately wished she could snatch the words back and swallow them down. Her voice was quiet, but the pitch of it was unmistakable—tender and confoundingly female.

But the older woman just shrugged, waved a hand in the direction of the house. "Inside," she said, her tone suddenly perfunctory, sapped of its honey. Her attention had already shifted to a man walking along the other side of the road.

Charity nodded, then made her way up the sagging steps of the front porch. She felt wholly separate from herself, sirened to this place as if possessed: the bird-boned fingers of a stranger reaching for the brass knocker on the door, rapping insistently until it swung open and Marie appeared.

Her face was scrubbed clean and she looked younger, her cheeks pink with the raw bloom of acne. Neither woman spoke for a moment and Charity felt a rush of panic at her foolishness, at the absurdity of her coming here. But then Marie's face cracked open into a smile. "Well, I'll be damned," she said. A few wisps of red hair had slipped free of their pins and they hung in her eyes, which were a murky green flecked with yellow. She was a strange-looking woman, her face soft and plump but cratered with scars, her eyes set wide apart, her freckled skin waxy and flour-white.

"Come inside," Marie said, her eyes searching Charity's, curious. She hooked a single finger into the belt loop of Charity's trousers and pulled, the soft tug of a question.

Charity stepped back, her face hot with embarrassment. She knew what men were supposed to come here for; she understood why Marie had beckoned her, what it meant when a person knocked on this door. But her pockets were empty, and any desire she had was nested deep within her, bound so tight that she didn't dare to imagine its unfurling.

Marie moved her hand away from Charity's waist and placed it gently on her shoulder. Her smile softened, widened, a door opening. "Come inside," she said again, but this time with a new warmth, somehow understanding.

Upstairs, Marie handled Charity's uneasiness as if it were a breakable thing, something fragile to cup between her palms. She sat far from her on the bed, letting Charity adjust to her proximity the way she might let a skittish cat sniff at her outstretched fingers, and talked to fill the space between them.

Marie had survived her own set of tragedies that had brought her to this place: her parents and sister had died of pneumonia when she was young, and she'd gone to live with an aunt who was herself destitute and desperate. They'd shared a single room above a tavern, and at night

Marie would retreat to the cool darkness beneath her blanket and press her hands over her ears, trying to drown out the sounds of the men who came upstairs for her aunt. Sometimes she'd be sent out into the hallway, where she'd curl up in front of the door and wait to be let back inside, tracing the imprint of boot soles on the dusty wood floors, touching her ear to the ground to listen to the creaking whine of the floorboards, the shouts of men in the bar below.

When Marie was fourteen, her aunt had moved them into this house and Marie had begun working as well, learning her worth in currency, learning the strange contours of desire. She paid dues to the women of the house who clothed her, fed her, sheltered her, and to her aunt for taking her in and offering her any life at all. Like Charity's, hers was a life hitched to the wants of other people.

Charity listened to Marie's stories, rapt as a child, and it was as if the seams of her began to unknit. She loosened into the space, lay back on the soft down of Marie's bed, closed her eyes to better imagine this version of Marie that hadn't always shimmered with life. And then she'd told her own story, surprised by the way her voice could fill the room. She rarely ever spoke, close to mute when she was in public, the slivers of communication between her and Maeve infrequent and treacherous. But talking to Marie, she'd felt relief crack open inside her with each revelation, and she'd let the whole truth unspool: tattered and threadbare, a snaking ribbon between them. Marie had known parts of it already, of course—understood the gist if not the specifics, recognized the way Charity branched apart at impossible angles.

"But how did you know?" Charity had asked. She often wondered what people saw when they looked at her, whether they sensed some otherness, some quiet duplicity. Sometimes she'd notice strangers studying her body or peering curiously at her face, as if scanning her for answers. Men at work occasionally snickered when she walked by, muttered things under their breath, unsure what to make of her. But it seemed to Charity that Marie had intuited her whole self right from the start.

Marie smiled. "I just knew there was more to you. You were different," she said, and leaned in a tiny bit closer. Then, as if registering some flicker of worry on Charity's face, she added, "Special, I mean. It made me want to know every part of you."

Charity looked down, heat rising to her cheeks, and it felt like she was somehow holding danger and safety in one hand: the reflexive fear of being found out, the unfamiliar comfort of being known.

*

Charity sits at Marie's dressing table, her stiffly pressed shirt unbuttoned at the neck, her hands folded in her lap. She glances at herself in the mirror, and the image glares out at her, disappointed and hateful. *Coward*, it murmurs silently. Her hair is matted down, stiff with spit, and the memory of Marie's hands combing through it is an ache: Marie licking her fingertips, pinching a tendril of Charity's hair, pressing it into a curl against Charity's cheek. Then, her tongue against the flat of her hand, licking from her wrist to the tips of her fingers. Running her palm through the hair across Charity's forehead. Smiling, her crooked teeth already so familiar to Charity, a glimpse into how the details of a person might start to feel like home. Charity has only ever known the intricacies of her mother, the intimate tangle of things that make her who she is—the whistle of her breath when she sleeps, the triangular constellation of birthmarks along her inner arm, the way one blue eye drifts, unmoored, when she drinks too much whiskey—but there is no comfort there. Maeve's presence has never felt like safety; it has never felt like home.

Marie and Charity had smiled at each other in the mirror then, giggled at Charity's hair, wet with spit, admired the clean division Marie had created: on one side, the oiled swoop of a man's haircut; on the other, tight spit curls in a cascade against the curve of her cheek. "See?" Marie had said, as if something had been proven, a debate put to rest.

"But which version of me do you like best?" Charity had asked, turning her head side to side, lighthearted but also desperate for an answer. *What if neither version of me is right?* she'd wanted to ask. *What then?*

"Both versions of you are perfect," Marie had said, and then the women had fallen silent, as if waiting for something—a force to draw them together, an interruption to pull them apart—and Charity could feel her fingers tingling with a new need: to reach for Marie, to feel the soft weight of her. How easy it would be, she thought, to close the space between them.

And then finally, mercifully, Marie's fingers grazed the skin of Charity's wrist, laddered up her arm. Marie's voice, throaty in Charity's ear, praising every part of her. "I think you're beautiful both ways." Her touch like an exquisite heat, a brand left on Charity's skin: *beautiful,*

beautiful, beautiful. But then, Charity's body pulling traitorously away. Ripping the delicate threads that had begun braiding between them. Leaving Marie holding on alone.

"I'm sorry," Charity whispers now, willing Marie to reach for her again. There is no way to explain herself, except to say that such bold kindness is foreign to her, that being cared for feels like its own transgression: a gift she doesn't deserve, a mutinous and misguided belief in her worth.

"Don't apologize," Marie says. "I think I've misunderstood." She smiles limply and stands, crosses to the door. "I should probably get back to work though." Her hand is on the knob, a gentle request, and her words are polite but charged: Charity has not been paying her for her time. They've spent nearly every afternoon together since they met, afternoons when Marie was supposed to be working, when the other women likely assumed she was working—that Charity was a patron like any other. She arrived each day as Charles, trailed Marie up the stairs with the bowed head of a man nervous to be seen here, sheepish about the implications of his visit.

Charity nods but doesn't move from the bench, waiting for the right words to come to her, words that will pull Marie back. She digs into her pockets; it's Friday, payday, and though Maeve will demand the money the moment she arrives home, Charity pulls it out and lays it on the dressing table. The amount is measly, surely not enough to cover their string of long afternoons, but she knows no other way to say what she means.

Marie stares at the crumpled bills for a moment, then turns the knob and clicks the door open. "You should keep your money," she says, her voice flat. Charity can hear the din of voices downstairs, a flutter of laughter.

Charity pushes the bills further onto the table, unable to look up at Marie. "I didn't mean to waste your time." The words feel like bile in her throat, so far from what she wants to say.

Marie reaches for the money on the table. "I can't keep this," she says, holding it out to Charity. "I've done nothing for you." Her eyes are a lightless, leaden green, and Charity can feel her slipping away: the space between them slackening, a spell breaking. Soon Marie will be more knowable to the nameless men who filter in and out of her room—men who know the rhythm of her body rather than just the rhythm of her voice. Men who are only men, who feel the truth of who they are solid and whole inside them. Who have not been halved down the middle and pulled in two directions until barely anything is left.

Charity stands and grabs her coat and hat from the foot of the bed. She buttons the top of her loosened shirt, reassembling the pieces of herself into someone who makes sense: a small man who shrinks from view, face shadowed by a cap pulled low. She slips into her coat and tugs the cap down over her ears, her fingers grazing the stiff whorl of spit curls plastered to her right cheek. She presses the palm of her hand to them for a moment, traces a curl with the tip of her finger, maps where Marie's wet fingers had brushed against her skin. Marie watches, her expression unreadable.

"Thank you," Charity says, and the words feel full, laden, but also entirely inadequate. She touches a finger to her tongue and presses it to the stiff curl, as if sealing it against her skin. She takes her hat off, holds it in one hand, uses the other to slick down the hair across her forehead. "I like them both too," she says. "Both sides." And then, finally, a choice. A blind step forward: she tosses the hat back onto the bed. It lands softly near Marie's pillow, and Marie lets out a surprised sound almost like a laugh. The women look over at the bed, the blank expanse of it, an open landscape.

"Charity," Marie says, and a warmth has returned to her voice, a teasing lilt. "You can't leave without your hat."

The women stare at each other for a moment, and the moment stretches out between them, bending with possibility. A dividing or a binding.

And then the corner of Marie's mouth quirks upward, not a smile exactly, but a silent proposal: *stay*.

Charity nods, pulls off her coat, and Marie crosses to her. A tentative hand outstretched, that hint of a smile, the glint of her lovely, crooked teeth, so perfect in their strangeness: an invitation to something like home.

CASTEJÓN DE EBRO

I watch their hands as they sit side by side: her fingers worrying the felt pad tucked beneath her beer glass, his tapping an impatient rhythm on the wood of the table top. They're polite to me and to each other but there's a tension in the air, a cord pulled tight, fraying, threatening to snap. They drink fast, too fast, and then they're ordering more; she's watching him and he's watching me, and I can tell he wants to impress us with his clumsy, broken Spanish. I pretend not to understand English so they'll speak freely, but their conversation has the stumbling cadence of strangers filling lost time. He whispers something to her and puts a hand on her knee, a tender gesture that raises goosebumps on my arms. She smiles uncertainly, a child aiming to please but unsure of the rules, and I stifle the unbidden impulse to mother her, to reach down and swat him away. Silence bloats and settles between them.

They keep drinking and when I return with a third round, I can see that the drinks have begun to dull their edges. They're drinking anís faster than it's meant to be drunk, saying things to each other in hushed tones meant to be shouted. I go back into the bar, light a cigarette and watch them through the lazy sway of the beaded curtain that separates us. They're staring at nothing, quiet again, their lips set in sad straight lines. In Castejón we bellow our anger and our love; we hit with our words and sometimes with the flat of our palms, but rarely with our silence. I blow a hot line of smoke out a cracked window above the bar and tighten the damp apron around my hips, but I don't go back outside. They're talking again: I can hear the even simmer of their voices, measured pleas churning between them without crescendo, tidy and aimless.

Then the man calls for another round in his halting Spanish, and his tone is less gentle than before, less about the ritual and more about the beer he wants to drink. I rinse two more glasses and fill them to the brim, and then I stand listening at the curtain with the beers in my hands, but the couple has gone quiet. Their train is coming soon, an express to Madrid, and I wonder for a moment what happens to the delicate inertia of two people careering toward a shared destination, when together they're going nowhere at all.

HOW TO GRIEVE THE LIVING

It was not the sort of story that could stay hidden in a small town. People in Florence paid attention to everyone else's details: a car missing from a driveway in the early morning hours, a skipped shift at work, one less body tucked into the pew on Sunday morning. This was how the people of Florence governed themselves: with the understanding that there was no such thing as a secret.

A line of police cars had shown up in front of the house a little after midnight—not just the local patrol cars that drove lazy circles around the surrounding farmland each day, but a county fleet—and by late morning the rumors had branched into the loose shape of a story. One neighbor had heard the gunshots; a man who'd been walking home from the bar, drunk and fuzzy on the details, swore he saw a body being rolled out of the house and down the walk. Several people noted that the unfamiliar car parked out front had been there all night. And no one who lived in the house had answered when the neighbors came by the next morning, one by one, to ring the bell and peer through the slender gap in the living room curtains.

Over the following week the details began to emerge in fragments, first as whispered approximations of the truth and then, finally, as solid facts about what had happened. But by then a separate mythology had grown around the house, digging in roots that couldn't be unearthed, snaking their way over the doors and across the windows, blotting out the light and choking the lives inside.

*

Before that night—the night of the Chestnut Street Murder, as it came to be known—Edith's life had been small and quiet. The child of gregarious parents whose sociability seemed to blunt any glimmer of her own, it often bewildered her that she could be the product of two people so different from herself. They were wild, raging fires; she was a delicate ribbon of smoke rising up between them, barely there at all.

The night had resembled one like any other at first: the house had hummed with the muted energy of everyday life as Edith and her parents had moved through the motions of their nighttime routine. Dinner plates were cleared and dishes were scrubbed and the radio clicked on in the kitchen. The dog was taken for his evening walk; the television sprang to life in the corner of the living room. Outside, the sun slipped behind the trees and the wind picked up, scattering leaves from a neatly raked pile in the front yard.

In the following days, Edith would return again and again to those simple details, the dull everydayness of them, and to the impossible fact that violence and horror could so easily exist in their midst. The mood in the house had changed slowly, as gradual as the rising sliver of moon in the sky and the sun's sifting descent: a creeping darkness that settled and remained.

Edith had been upstairs with her mother when the man arrived at their house. She was lying back against the satin pillows of her parents' bed, flipping absently through a magazine and watching her mother in the mirror as she untwirled curlers from her hair. Helen's beauty regimen was elaborate and precise, a ritual so consistent that Edith sometimes wondered what her mother would look like were she ever to reverse the steps or forget to use one of the lotions that lined her dressing table. Helen smiled at herself in the mirror as she rubbed a fingerful of cold cream into her cheeks and then blotted them with a thick tissue that smelled of baby powder. She lifted a glass of gin to her lips and took a long sip, then reached for a makeup pencil and began drawing thin wisps of blond where her eyebrows ought to be. Edith touched a finger to her own brows, thick but an invisible white-blond like her hair, which hung long and pin-straight down her back. Helen forbade her to cut or dye it, not because of any motherly principles, but simply because it was important to her that Edith be beautiful.

Helen tugged at the metal clasps on her slip, lengthening the straps so the lace edging hung loose over her breasts and exposed the blush of her nipples. She made no move to cover herself, perhaps because the gin had begun to go her head, or perhaps because she enjoyed the image reflected back to her: a woman nearing forty whose body still unapologetically invited attention, whose breasts had somehow remained as round and pert as her teenage daughter's.

She spritzed perfume onto each wrist and along the curve of her neck, then sprayed a puff into the air and leaned into it, eyes closed like she was coming in for a kiss. She uncapped a new lipstick, slightly darker than her usual pink and harsh against her bone-white skin, and the change felt unsettling to Edith. There was a comfort to the way Helen looked, a tidy predictability to Edith's otherwise mercurial mother.

Helen stood then, reaching for the silk robe that hung on a hook beside her dressing table. She wrapped it around herself and studied her reflection, pulling at the sash around her waist so that the fabric gaped open to reveal the lace neckline of her slip. Then she parted the robe at her thighs, offering a flash of her slender legs, white as the creamy silk of her robe, and pulled a cigarette from a pack on the dressing table.

"Okay, Edie," she said, lighting the cigarette and blowing a thin line of smoke toward the mirror, her eyes still on her own reflection as she spoke. "Time to split."

Edith watched her mother posing, fussing with the hem of her robe, fingering the pearl pendant at her chest. "Aren't you going to get dressed?" Edith asked.

Helen's eyes flashed to Edith in the mirror. "Aren't *you*?" she responded, nonsensically, since Edith was still wearing her school uniform from earlier in the day. Helen took another sip of her drink, draining what was left of it, and ran her fingers through the limp waves of her hair. She had the same straight, cornsilk hair as Edith, though she used an arsenal of sprays and tools to coerce it into the loose curls she admired in the magazines beside her bed. "I told you to scoot," she said. Her words were beginning to bleed into each other and she seemed unsteady as she slipped her feet into a pair of high heels. "We're having a friend over for drinks."

As if on cue, Edith heard the sound of voices downstairs, low and muffled, and the creak of the floorboards in the front hall. Earlier that afternoon Helen had tried without subtlety to get rid of Edith for the evening, offering her money to see a movie, to take her friends out for milkshakes, to play the arcade. But Edith had already seen the movie playing at the Odeon and her friendships were flimsy, conditional—she rarely saw her friends outside of school. And she hated the arcade, her left hand stubbornly dominant despite her teachers' insistence that she rely on her right; the result seemed to be that neither hand worked properly anymore. Whenever she went to the arcade she'd lose every game in under a minute, releasing the flippers on the pinball machine at all the wrong moments, knocking skeeballs against the sides of the track and sending them bouncing across the floor.

She preferred to retreat to the attic room on these nights, the only space in the house where her parents allowed her to stay when they entertained their friends. She rarely got to see the friends her parents had over, and when she did they were never people she knew. Florence was a small town where lives overlapped: Edith's piano teacher also played organ at the church and waited tables at the diner; her dentist coached the school's baseball team and played poker with her father on Wednesdays. When Edith went with her mother to the supermarket, the woman ringing up their groceries would hand Helen a list of her latest Mary Kay products and later come over to the house so Helen could sample them. There were very few strangers in Florence, but the friends who came to visit her parents were not people who Edith later spotted in the seats behind her at church or cheering on their kids at a high school football game. They appeared and then disappeared, leaving behind empty glasses coated in the grainy dregs of red wine, cigarette stubs stamped with lipstick, stale air thick with unfamiliar cologne.

After everything happened, a police officer had asked Edith questions about the man who'd come over that night—*how had her parents met him, why had be been at the house*—but Edith could only stare at the officer blankly, her eyes drifting to the scalloped edges of a gold pendant on his lapel, the starched angles of his shirt cuffs, the way the white buttons of his uniform glinted like opals under the harsh lights of the precinct.

She knew nothing about the man who'd come to their house, nothing about how he'd met her parents or how her parents knew any of the other people they invited over on the weekends. She understood in a distant, shapeless way what happened on these late nights— nights when her parents stood at the stove together, her mother cooking rushed meals with a wine glass in hand, her father tracing his fingers down Helen's spine like he was playing an instrument, the air tight and charged between them until the doorbell rang and they shooed Edith upstairs. Edith filed these nights away with all the other puzzles of adulthood, wondering only vaguely if other high school parents spent their weekends this way. She'd never witnessed anything beyond a handful of strange moments—her parents slow-dancing in the living room paired with other people, her father standing in front of his record collection with a man she'd never seen before, the cigarette between his fingers held to the other man's lips.

Then the officer had asked for her account of the night's events, though surely he knew from the report that Edith had been found in the attic crawlspace, nearly catatonic, her body folded into the impossibly small pocket of darkness behind the stairs. It had been a favorite hiding spot during childhood: an instant victory in games of hide and seek, a respite when the fragile alchemy of her parents' marriage started to turn poisonous. That night, she'd hidden in the crawlspace for what felt like hours before the police finally found her there, her hands sealed tight over her ears to drown out whatever horrors she'd heard bellowing up from below.

It had been her mother's screams she'd heard first. She'd been stretched out across the threadbare couch tucked under the eaves in the attic, a book spread across her lap. She'd just begun to drift off—she often slept there on weekend nights, not bothering to sneak back down to her bedroom when she heard the front door slam shut or a car pull away from their house. The sound of her mother screaming had ripped up through the floor, rising above the deep thump of music playing downstairs, pulling Edith from her half-sleep. Then, the sickening crack of gunfire: three bangs in rapid succession followed by a final shot so loud it seemed to thread through her and settle in her bones. She'd dropped to the ground and pried open the door to the crawlspace, the shots ringing in her ears and arrowing through her like a vein of electricity long after the house had turned still and quiet.

*

Whenever something bad happened in Florence, there was a ritual that people followed, a formalized response to tragedy: weeks of meals that kept well, packaged to stack neatly in a freezer, labeled with simple instructions requiring no thought and no labor; assistance offered wordlessly and invisibly so that trashcans somehow found their way to the curb each week and lawns managed to never creep above two inches.

But when Edith and Helen returned home after everything happened, finally allowed back into their house by police after more than a week spent in a cheap motel two towns over, people in town kept their distance. They regarded the mother and daughter with a hesitant curiosity, as if the women were wild animals who hadn't yet revealed whether they were tame or feral. Because theirs wasn't the sort of tragedy people understood. Helen hadn't lost her husband to sickness or an accident. Edith's father hadn't been killed heroically overseas. They were not bereaved, shadowed instead by a different kind of creature.

At first, Edith tried going back to school, hoping to exist on the social fringes the way she always had. She was shy and pretty and bookish, a combination that had allowed her to fly under the radar with a small circle of similarly unobjectionable girls, not popular but also not targeted. They weren't the girls who got invited to parties, but they weren't the ones getting cruel notes shoved into their lockers and rumors written about them in bathroom stalls either.

But back at school, she found that she'd lost the power to disappear: the hum of whispers hung in the air around her like radio static, eyes boring into her with unveiled disdain. Hardly anyone talked to her but they all talked around her, muttering versions of the truth; the most brazen among them announced their accusations loud enough for her to hear, saying that her father was a homo and her mother was a whore, that her parents threw sex parties, that her house was actually a brothel. Even the few friends she had at school ignored her, placing stacks of textbooks on the extra seats at their lunch table on her first day back, staring wordlessly down at their food as Edith stood, confused, waiting for them to make room for her. After a week of sitting alone at lunch, of studiously ignoring the sneers and whispers, Edith arrived at school to find the word *SLUT* scraped deep into the metal of her locker. A note had been tucked into one of the vents—*Like mother like daughter*. She stopped using her locker after that and carried her books from class to class instead, but by then she'd already been branded, as if the ragged edge of a key had scraped the word into her skin as well. In her English class a few days later, Edith found a note folded into a tight square and placed on her desk. When she opened it, she immediately recognized the romantic sweep of her friend Betsy's penmanship beneath a drawing of a stick figure holding a knife in one hand and a gun in the other. *My name is Edie! I live in a whorehouse and you'll probably get murdered, but want to come for a slumber party?* Laughter erupted from the back of the room, and Edith decided she was done with school.

"Good riddance to that place," Helen said flatly when Edith came home and told her mother that she'd decided to quit and take the high school equivalency exam. At barely fourteen years old, Edith had no idea if this was even allowed—usually the drop-outs were older, either pregnant or leaving school to work for their families. She'd never known someone to simply quit.

Helen was stretched out across her bed, still in her nightgown even though it was nearly four in the afternoon. She'd moved the television into her bedroom a few days earlier and detritus had begun piling up on the unused side of the bed: dirty plates and silverware, empty cartons of cigarettes, unopened mail, a collection of miniature gin bottles that clinked accusingly every time she moved. She pulled a lighter from the pocket of her nightgown and patted the crumpled sheets around her until she found a loose cigarette. Lighting it, she said, "Tommy was the one who cared about all that school stuff anyway." She exhaled a thread of smoke and turned her attention back to the television.

Helen had begun referring to Edith's father in the past tense—*Tommy handled the finances, Tommy always made sure there was gas in the car, Tommy loved that song*—and it made something tighten inside Edith, a fist of sadness that squeezed and held on. She'd always felt a little uneasy around her father; Tommy was a big personality, the loudest person in every room, and he and Edith never knew quite what to make of each other. When they were alone together they lapsed into exaggerated versions of themselves, Edith shrinking mutely away, Tommy expanding into the space as if he were performing a one-man show. But without him, the house felt hollowed out, sapped of something vital. His absence was itself a presence; the loss was a beast that descended on them, gnawed away at Edith and picked Helen clean.

Helen looked up at Edith, her eyes shadowy and vacant. "You can drive, right?"

Edith blinked. "I..."

"Tommy taught you, didn't he? Enough to get around?" She seemed suddenly impatient, as if they'd been having a conversation about this and Edith was being uncooperative.

Edith shrugged. "He let me practice in the church parking lot a couple times. I can't... I haven't driven on the road or anything."

Helen tapped her cigarette against the lip of a glass. The water inside had turned a murky gray, thick with ash from the day's cigarettes. "I just need you to take his car to the lot in town. See what you can get for it."

Edith hesitated. "Like... try to sell it?"

Helen's face darkened and she turned her gaze away from Edith. "It's not like he's going to need it." Eyes fixed on the television and her skin bathed in the flickering glow of the screen, she said, "He's going to rot in that place, Edie. He isn't ever getting out."

The words were a knife twisting in Edith's gut, slicing cleanly through all the whispered reassurances, the empty comforts that had gotten her and Helen through the past few weeks—*the lawyers will get him out, the police will realize they've got it wrong, he'll prove it was self-defense, he's innocent, he's innocent, he has to be innocent.* The words tore through fragile tissue, splintered through Edith's bones to the bloody truth of it: her father had killed a man and dismantled his own family with four pulls of a trigger. He'd chosen this—chosen it four times—and left them to survive in the wreckage.

*

Nat's was about a mile down the road, a two-car repair shop shouldered by parking lots full of old cars that shimmered like scales in the sunlight. Banners announcing low prices and cash for parts flapped along the perimeter and an old marquee sat at the entrance to the lot, faded letters set at odd angles like crooked teeth: *WE BUY SED CAR*. A sun-bleached sign boasting an Independence Day sale fluttered on a flagpole all year long.

Even though the lot was a straight shot from the house, Edith drove her father's car at a crawl, afraid to shift into second gear without Tommy there to wrap her small hand in his and gently guide the gearshift into place like a doctor setting a bone. By the time Edith arrived at the used car lot, the steering wheel was slick with sweat and she could feel the flicker of her heartbeat in her palms as if she were cupping a living thing between them. She had never quite mastered the delicate footwork of driving her father's car, never learned the graceful maneuver of shifting from one gear to the next.

You just gotta feel it, Edie, her father would say whenever the car stalled out and she asked him to explain to her precisely what it was her feet were supposed to do. It was as if the car were revolting against her, shuddering its resistance—a wild horse bucking under weakness, refusing to be broken by a fearful rider.

Each pedal needs something a little different, same as people, her father had said.

But Edith understood people about as well as she understood cars, stamping down on the pedals and shifting at random and hoping she'd end up in the right gear, say the right thing, laugh at the right moment. Her father did these things without thought or effort; when he entered a room, the space grew around him, lungs expanding to breathe him in. When he slipped back into the driver's seat to take Edith home after a driving lesson, the car would relax under his touch, suddenly a smooth and elegant thing, a different animal altogether.

Nat was standing out front when Edith arrived, shielding his eyes with the back of his arm and watching, bemused, as the car quaked to a stop between two painted parking spaces. He was the reason Edith was there, two years shy of a driver's license, with her father's paperwork in a tidy pile on the passenger's seat. According to Helen, Nat wouldn't think twice about buying a jailed man's car off a fourteen-year-old girl. *Nathaniel Evans would steal a ten-dollar watch from a corpse*, she'd said, handing Edith Tommy's key ring. *Just keep your distance. He loves a pretty little thing almost as much as he loves easy money.*

Nat was handsome in a dirty, sun-roughened way, his large hands black with grease, fingernails edged in grime. As Edith climbed out of the car, he took her in with a half-smile that felt to her like an appraisal of its own. She tucked her hair behind her ears and clutched the car's paperwork to her chest, trying to meet Nat's eyes as he came toward her.

"Well, would you look at this sunflower that just sprouted up in my parking lot," he said, clapping his hands together. "To what do I owe the pleasure?" He gave her a wide smile and she noticed that his front teeth slanted inward, overlapping like crossed legs, and it made him look playful somehow, boyish. The effect was disarming, and she felt herself smiling back at him.

She tilted her head toward the car. "My, uh... this is my dad's car. He's..." she trailed off, unsure how to explain the tangle of events that had brought her there.

But Nat just nodded, reaching for the pile of papers in her hands. "Got it. Say no more." He looked over at the car, then squinted down at the papers. "Just tell me if we're fixing it or selling it or both."

Edith felt a rush of relief at not having to explain herself or the situation, at not having to make a case for why he should buy a car from a teenager. "It runs fine, I think," she told him with a shrug. "We just don't need it anymore."

Nat looked up from what the paperwork. "Edie, right?" he asked. "Your daddy always talked about you like you were a little kid, but look at you all grown."

"It's actually Edith now," she said reflexively, then worried that perhaps she sounded rude. But she hated the nickname, so cute and peppy, so guileless. Edie felt to her like a pat on the head.

"Roger that. Edith. Guess I haven't talked to Tommy in a while." Then something shifted in his face, a cloud passing in front of the sun. "Look, I..." He hesitated. "I'm sorry about all the ugliness that's going on right now. With your dad. I'm sure it's been hell."

Edith cleared her throat, unsure what to say. She looked down at the cracked pavement at their feet, at the stubbled weeds pushing their way between the cement seams, incongruous and hopeful.

"Tommy was a real good guy," Nat continued. "I don't know what in the hell happened. I just know he was a good, honest guy." He winked at her. "And that's coming from someone who doesn't make a habit of complimenting anybody who ain't pretty and single."

Edith smiled uncertainly. *He loves a pretty little thing almost as much as he loves easy money.*

"Anyway," he said, turning back to the car, as if suddenly remembering why she was there. He walked over to the passenger's side and tucked the stack of papers under the windshield wipers. "Why don't you leave her here for me to take a look at, and then you can come by tomorrow after school so we can square up."

Edith paused. "I don't go to school," she told him, trying out the words for the first time. She liked the feel of them, crisp and definitive—not the soft, round sounds of a child asking permission.

Nat pulled a pack of Lucky Strikes from his back pocket. "That so?" he asked, shaking a cigarette loose. "How'd that come to be?" A lighter hissed between his fingers as he lit the cigarette and exhaled a clean line of smoke.

"I'd rather get a job now that my dad's gone." It was only a half-formed thought, an idea that had just begun to edge its way in, but saying it to Nat made it feel real, factual.

He nodded, unfazed, and she wondered what other realities she could speak into existence. She looked at the cigarette pinched between his fingers. "Can I have one of those?" she asked. She'd smoked a handful of times before and had never liked it much. It made her feel lightheaded and a little sick. But every part of her felt different now, as if over the past few weeks everything had been rearranged: stretches of hollow bone in places that used to be tender, nerves nested deep, heart replaced by some other muscle, a lump of something harder.

"I quit school around your age too," Nat said, taking out the pack and tapping it against his palm. "But I did it to get out of my house. Both my parents were in and out of jail and my brother was a piece of shit. I just wanted to be on my own." Nat pulled out another cigarette, but instead of handing it to her, he put it into his own mouth and lit it with the one he'd been smoking. Then he held it out, the burning end pointed away from her, and she took it between her lips. The act felt intimate, as if they were sharing in some sort of sacred ritual, and he held her gaze until she looked away.

They smoked in silence for a bit, looking out over the lot of cars, each one fitted with a handwritten sign behind the front windshield. The sun was beginning to set in the distance, glinting off the cars' metal roofs, and it occurred to Edith that she'd made no plan for how to get home. At this rate she'd be walking back along a pitch-black highway.

"So," Nat said, turning back to her. "You talked to your daddy since all this happened?"

The question surprised Edith, and she took a hard pull on her cigarette. She'd once heard her father say that the best way to get to know someone was to have a smoke with them. *People open up when they have something in common and something to do*, he'd said. *And it helps if they don't even have to look at each other.*

"I've seen him a few times," she said. It was true that talking felt easier with something in her hand, the clouds of smoke between them a reason to look the other direction. "I didn't go the last time my mom visited though. I just... I don't like seeing him in there." The image of her father flashed through her mind, pale and diminished even though he'd been in for less than a month, his eyes dark, hollowed out. He'd seemed defeated, as if he already knew exactly how all of this was going to go. "I don't think he's gonna get out though," she said, her mother's voice like a ringing in her ear, dull but persistent. *He's going to rot in that place, Edie. He isn't ever getting out.*

Nat studied her for a moment. "I'm real sorry to hear that, Edith. I know it's a complicated situation, with your parents having an unusual lifestyle and all." He paused. "Sorry, I don't mean any offense by that. I just hear what I hear."

Edith felt her breath catch in her throat and a numbness start to throb in her fingertips, like her body trying to armor itself limb by limb. This had been happening to her ever since her dad's arrest, a tingling panic that coursed through her at the mention of that night, of her parents' marriage, of whatever it was they were doing that led to a man getting killed. She cleared her throat. "I don't know what happened," she said, taking a deep breath and hoping that would put an end to whatever conversation he was trying to have. "I don't know anything about all that."

He shook his head. "No, no, I know. Sorry. I wasn't trying to pry. I just..." He ran his hands through his hair and she wondered if she'd managed to fluster him. "I know it's hard, is all. Seeing him like that. Hearing people talk. Figuring out how to feel about him after all this." He looked straight at her, and she noticed that in the fading sunlight his eyes were a loose, honeyed color, brown veined in gold. Kind and gentle. *Nathaniel Evans would steal a ten-dollar watch from a corpse.* She didn't respond, so he went on. "Once I left home for good, it was easier to just forget them. My folks. Everybody I'd known before."

"How did you do that?" Edith asked. She imagined what it would be like to willfully forget the past—to scrub clean the thought of her father, hands cuffed together as if in prayer. Her mother in bed, broken and unmoored. Nights when their house swirled with smoke and music and she was warned not to come downstairs under any circumstances, not unless the attic was on fire. Jeers and rumors and *SLUT* carved into her locker.

"I just thought of them as already gone. Learned how to grieve the living, I guess. Pretended they weren't out there in the world." Nat dropped his cigarette to the ground and crushed it under his boot, then kicked it away. "God's honest truth, it's what I did with my wife and kid too."

Edith looked at him in surprise. "You're married?" she asked. Her memories of what she knew about Nat were blurry, the sort of shapeless knowledge that came from hearing slivers of other people's conversations. She didn't remember him having a family.

"I was. My ex left with our kid years ago, and that was that. She ran off, and six months later I got served with papers." He shrugged, but his expression was dark. "I don't even know how old my son would be. Can't let myself do that math. Once they were gone, I… well, I had to sorta kill them in my mind. Sounds messed up, but it is what it is. Easier than knowing they're out there without me."

Edith didn't know how to respond. She'd never thought of absence as a kind of death, never considered how all the people she'd met but never seen again were, within her own private world, as good as dead. She could refuse to see her father and grieve him as if he were gone, instead of allowing him this feeble half-life.

Or she could just leave. She looked at her father's car in front of them, at the stack of papers tucked beneath its wipers, the keys resting on its hood. She could grab the keys and climb in without explanation, drive in the opposite direction of her house, keep driving. Leave her mother suspended in their final moment together, her warning about Nat the last piece of motherly advice she'd ever give. Edith could end her father's life in that hot visitation room, snuff out the lives of everyone she'd ever known, light this town on fire by leaving it forever. Maybe forgetting was just a gentler way of killing them all.

WHAT WE IMAGINED

Before the walls collapsed, they were vast and full of color. We lost our security deposit the day we moved in—Evie slathered the hallways with blues and yellows, painted roses along the window panes so the morning sun cast squares of red light across the tiles of our kitchen. In the beginning, her paintings made the world swing wide open; our tiny house became infinite. She painted on everything: her shoes, old jam jars and empty tissue boxes, the handles of cabinets and the ledge of the bathtub. At night I'd stare up at the ceiling of our bedroom, inky blue peppered with orange, stabs of light in a faraway cosmos. The walls of the living room were pages of fairytales and sleeves of tattoos; they yawned open and ushered us inside, told us their stories, showed us how wide and pliable space can be.

"I'm not permanent," she'd said to me the day we met. She'd been assigned the cubicle across from mine and had slid her chair across the aisle, twirling to face me like a kid playing in her dad's office. I knew she was a temp; there was a new person every month or so.

"That's unfortunate," I said, and she smiled.

That night she took me to her apartment and showed me stacks of photographs she'd taken of her work. It took me a moment to realize I was looking at human bodies, at paint on skin: the fiery eye of a dragon was actually a man's belly button; the scalloped wings of a butterfly were the smooth expanse of a woman's inner thigh. I asked her to paint me and she said she was afraid. "You're already so closed off," she said, stroking a dry paintbrush along the curve of my ear. "What if the paint seals you up completely?"

After a few weeks in the house Evie painted our bedroom walls a milky, underwater blue, and that's when they began to breathe. I'd watch them expand like lungs, the blue stretching tight as the skin of a balloon and then releasing, puckering with a faint *whiiiiish*. At night she cooked strange, exotic meals from the pages of a cookbook left by the tenants before us. Veils of smoke the color of turmeric and cardamom would lift from the stove and the porous walls would spread open, pump the spices into the kitchen and through the hallways and down into our throats; the house fed us, left us full and intoxicated. Some nights I'd try to help, gingerly stirring soup when she turned away or peering into the oven to check on a rising loaf of bread, looking for ways to create something alongside her. But she always shooed me out or swatted me away, just as she did when I tried to watch her paint. She was building this all on her own.

Later, we'd curl up in our bed under a pile of blankets and I'd wrap myself around her. Her limbs were long and full of hard angles, her body difficult to hold onto. She often pushed me aside after sex, creating space between us in the moments when I craved more of her.

When she'd painted our bedroom, the blue paint had dripped down over the vents and dried there like a seam, and after that the room was always cold; still, most nights she rolled away from me.

The collapse was slow and incremental. She was offered a spot in a gallery show downtown; she quit the temp agency; she told me I needed to quit my office job. The gallery was paying her almost nothing, the commission eating the price down so low that her take-home pay would barely cover the cost of supplies once the paintings sold. She had two pieces on display: a chaotic abstract on a 4×4 canvas, moody and abrasive, and a delicate, meticulous oil painting the size of a postcard. I laughed at her when she said that this was my chance to leave the business world behind—that we could survive on art alone—and in that moment something broke between us. The night of the gallery opening she drank too much free wine and when we got home she told me the suit I was wearing repulsed her, that my life was artless and my tolerance for mediocrity would one day devour me. I slammed the bedroom door in her face and it cried out like a child, vibrated like the string of a guitar. The vibration rippled through the walls, a quiet undertow rumbling beneath the surface. When she crawled into bed with me hours later, I was the one to slide away.

After that, the house began to change. Evie kept painting it but there was a flatness to her work; she sketched a family of mice skittering into a hole in the wall, and each day I watched them for signs of life, waiting for one of them to dart across the floor in front of me or grow plump with crumbs from our kitchen floor. But for weeks they remained inanimate until one day I came home from work and they were gone, streaks of gray as faint as shadows where her drawing once had been.

I couldn't help but notice that at some point the walls had slowed their breathing as well—that they could often go days without drawing a single breath. Around the same time, the living room ran out of stories to tell.

I'd sit on the couch and wait for the murals to part like the curtains of a stage, but most days the room remained quiet and still. When Evie and I lay in our bed at night, all that was left was the thrum of the world outside; there was no music pulsing from the floorboards, no wind whistling through painted trees or stars shooting wildly across the universe she'd built above us. Our house was becoming a husk of itself, nothing more than slabs of wood covered in approximate renditions of life, windows painted over to keep the light out.

And then one day it was gone. I woke up and the walls of our bedroom had contracted around us, so close to my face that for a moment I thought maybe my eyes were still shut, that the wash of blue before me was imagined. I could breathe, but just barely, and out of the corner of my eye I could make out a slash of white beside me, Evie's pale body stark against the tangle of blankets. She was taking quick, panicked breaths, as if air were something she could store up and save for later. I tried to speak but no sound came out, my mouth thick with texture, something unnameable filtering down my throat and expanding in my belly. I could feel the texture swell inside me, spreading to my organs, prodding at my insides. I didn't try to reach out and touch Evie; even as the walls pushed further in, closing up around us like a wound healing over, we found enough room to be separate.

When the colors parted I could see the space where the door used to be, its edges knit tightly together, closing us off from where the rest of the house had stood the night before. The textures were shifting their form above us, the blues of our bedroom eclipsed by pockets of color from the living room, snapshots of the stories Evie had painted into existence.

Vultures snapped at our faces and a pinup girl wrapped in an American flag slowly disrobed, her cartoonish nipples popping out from behind the folds of fabric. A child emerged from a copse of trees and her mouth opened into the perfect circle of a scream, a circle that widened more and more until it felt as if she might swallow us whole.

A knot of acrylic roses crept up my torso and wrapped tight around my neck, and beside me the limbs of a tree cracked our bed in half and an eddy of crisp leaves churned between us. The silhouette of a wolf landed hard on my chest and his howl emerged, shuddering and primal, from somewhere deep in my throat. I could hear Evie howling beside me and above us the moon rose up round and silver, beckoning our pack of two, casting its net around us. We rolled toward each other and it was as if we'd been threaded onto a single spool; for an instant, I understood the symbiotic power that exists between the moon and its creatures. She smiled at me and I reached for her, but then she was gone, wisps of color dissolving between my fingertips. And then the wolf too was gone, replaced by a tiny starling that chirped sweetly in my cupped palms, whose gentle heft was suddenly the only thing I knew to be true, the silk of its quivering wings as real or imagined as the rest of the world around us.

LET'S LET GO

Yours are fingers that pluck guitar strings and tumble over piano keys, that grab my hair in fistfuls, gentle but urgent, and draw heat to the surface of my skin. These are fingers that could someday weave double-knots into the shoelaces of our future children's shoes and smooth bandaids over their broken skin. These fingers cracked me open when I'd tried to seal my edges shut; they'd squeezed my cold hands and held on tight. Together, our palms had pulsed messages back and forth, silent proclamations, and back then a voiceless love had seemed like enough.

Then the priest had bound our wrists with ribbon, an ancient Irish ritual that I'd found romantic until I looked down at our tethered selves, an angry knot between us.

Later, I kneel in the same church that tied us to each other. I press my palms together, my fingertips directing questions to the sky. The priest volleys our questions back to us, and I turn them over in my hands as if maybe the answers are etched into my skin. He tells us that God would not create a rock so heavy He couldn't carry it. I try to hold onto this idea, but it slips through my threaded fingers and I leave with my hands empty at my sides.

Now, we still pass messages back and forth, but our hands speak different languages. I say *We'll get through this*, but it translates to *Something is broken*. I say *I love you*, but our hands are barely touching and the words are conjugated wrong: *I loved you.* I ask *Do you still love me?* but my palms are slick with sweat and the words slide away, never delivered at all. So instead I ask *Have we created something so heavy we can no longer carry it?*

And then we let go, fingers untwining, or maybe it's lives untwining, a ribbon unspooling until all that's left is the phantom press of something that's no longer there.

NEW SKIN

It started as little nicks on his arms, beads of blood he couldn't explain.

"Maybe you rubbed up against something thorny," his wife said, running her fingers over his stippled skin, rubbing away the blood to get a better look. "Were you working in the yard?" Beneath her fingers, the streaks of red looked like the wispy tails of dying stars.

That night, he washed his arm in the shower over and over, watched dots of blood rise to the surface each time, pinpricks that never released more than a tiny bubble of red. The punctures were scattered uniformly across his skin, shimmering like jewels on the faded tattoo that wreathed his arm.

It was the first tattoo he'd ever gotten—a ragged thing pressed into his skin with a fountain pen and sewing needle back in high school, a friend's approximation of barbed wire. The ink had spread out over the years, pooling in the knots of wire where the needle had gone in deepest, branching off from the once-straight lines like tiny channels cutting away from the twist of a river. For a long time it had been his favorite tattoo, a guaranteed conversation-starter. *Lemme tell you about the night my friend and I got bombed and gave each other tats in my parents' basement*, he'd say, lifting his shirtsleeve. *My buddy's got so infected we thought they were gonna have to chop his arm off.*

It was a story that got laughs and a round of *oh, shits*. It put people at ease with its happy ending—*Mike's still got all his limbs!*—and invited them to ask for more. *How'd you get that one?* and *What's the story there?* His body was a book they could open to any page.

But recently, his wife had asked him to stop showing it off to people. They'd been at a neighborhood barbecue and he'd pulled his sleeve up as usual, told the story the way he always did, ending with a crowdpleaser: *Now someone grab me a pen and a sewing kit so we can get this party started.* On the walk home, Theresa joked that maybe it was time to retire that story. She'd said this with a laugh, then turned immediately solemn. *But seriously, Ray,* she said. *Enough about the homemade tattoo.*

It wasn't because she was embarrassed, she'd insisted. It was a funny story. But it made him seem a little irresponsible, didn't it? They had a kid. They had a mortgage. They were trying to make a good impression on their new neighbors. Guys with kids and mortgages in nice neighborhoods didn't brag about their stick and poke tattoos.

*

A few days after his arm stopped bleeding, Ray woke up in the middle of the night, certain that the bed was on fire. He threw himself to the floor, pawing at the air around him, searching for the spread of flames. He pulled off his undershirt and pressed his palms to his chest. The heat rising from his body bit at his hands, and he heard the wet hiss of burning skin. Threads of smoke ribboned up between his fingers as the pain dissolved to an ache, and he ran a thumb gently over the tender flesh of his chest. Except it didn't feel like flesh, exactly. He stared down at his naked torso, at the dragon coiled along his sternum—a celebratory tattoo from the end of his time in the Marines—and pressed a little harder. The skin beneath his fingertips reminded him of the shells of the blister beetles he plucked off eggplants in the garden, slick and smooth as marbles.

"What the fuck," he murmured, tracing the tight curl of the dragon's tail, the braid of its scales, once a bright green now frothy with age. His skin had cooled but the texture still felt strange, wrong, as if the burn had immediately gummed to a scar that felt—*was he losing it?*—the way he imagined the flank of a dragon might feel.

He stood up, unsure what to do. Theresa was working the overnight shift at the hospital, and for a moment he considered bundling their daughter into the car and driving to the ER. But what would he say? That after a week of spontaneous bleeding, stubborn and insignificant as the drip of a leaky faucet, he'd begun feeling the phantom horror of his body on fire? That, while there was no sign of a burn, it did seem that his chest was scaling over and beginning to resemble the—*Jesus Christ, he was definitely going crazy*—skin of a dragon.

He flipped on the light and stood in front of the mirror, examining the tattoo on his chest: it was large and a little cartoonish, inked by a guy on the Ocean City boardwalk, but the sharp flare of the dragon's nostrils, blooming with flames that crawled up toward Ray's neck, made it slightly unnerving.

Put your shirt on, daddy, Poppy, his four-year-old, had demanded at the pool a few weeks earlier, eyeing his bare chest. *I don't want to see him.* She'd pointed a chubby finger at the dragon, then scowled up at her father. *I don't want my daddy to be scary.*

Her words had needled their way into him, carved away at some fragile place only his child could reach, and he'd spent the rest of the afternoon swimming in a t-shirt and worrying about what parts of him might frighten her next: the lion pouncing across his shoulder blades, the skull resting in the crook of his forearm, the wolf howling at a silvery moon on his back. As he spun his daughter in the water, watching the frantic kick of her little legs beneath the surface, he thought about all the creatures he was supposed to shield her from—all the beasts it was his job to defeat. Fatherhood meant being the lion tamer; he wasn't supposed to be one of the lions.

*

Ray was at the movies when things started to really get weird. There had been nearly a week of relative calm—an occasional twinge beneath his skin, tics of movement along its inked surface, one night when his muscles seized tight as a fist under the adder on his calf—and he'd pretty much accepted that it was a fluke he'd never understand, like a mysterious sickness that resolves on its own. But then, in the dark of a full movie theater, his body launched a new sort of mutiny.

First, a flutter that felt like fingertips tickling him from the inside. A vibration on the seat beneath him, so plain that he got up to inspect the cushion. And then, when he sat back down, a muffled voice rising up from under him, unmistakeable: the baritone lilt of a man singing.

Theresa looked over at him. She glanced at the seats behind them, then gave him a puzzled look. "What is that?" she whispered. The previews were over and a rustling hush had settled over the audience.

"You hear it too?" Ray asked, peering between the seat cushions. He bent down to scan the ground, though the distinct, rhythmic thrum in the seat of his pants was sending an arrow of panic through him. The sensation in his boxers—which felt like the patter of tiny, dancing feet along the curve of his ass, if he was being honest—was in perfect time with the rise and fall of the tinny voice belting up from underneath him.

Theresa studied him for a moment, then glanced down at his seat. "Are you messing with me?"

Ray regarded his wife, wondering how honest he should be with her. She looked tired but pretty, dressed up for their rare night out. Her hair hung in loose waves around her face and she'd applied dark eyeliner, an elegant swoop along the corner of each eye that made her look severe, feline, slightly pissed off.

"I'm not messing with you," he whispered, and that was all he could bring himself to say. The words that needed to come next felt like an impossible jumble of sounds, absurd in their simplicity: *But I'm pretty sure that Looney Tunes frog tattoo you hate is performing a musical number across my butt cheeks.*

He turned to face the movie screen, determined to ignore what was happening inside his pants and enjoy himself, to focus on the things he knew to be real. He took his wife's hand in his, soothed by the flicker of her pulse against his palm, her soft, placid skin. But the images and voices onscreen were already a blur of nonsense to him, eclipsed by the growing volume of musical notes repeated over and over again, like a record that kept snagging in the same groove. Ray readjusted himself and the notes grew louder, as if he'd opened up a pocket of space and the song was bellowing through it. The words rang out then, crisp and jaunty: *"Hello my baby, hello my honey, hello my ragtime gal..."*

Theresa turned to stare at him. "Raymond," she hissed. "You need to turn off whatever the hell is playing that music."

"Send me a kiss by wire, baby my heart's on fire..."

Ray looked at his wife, at the angry set of her jaw, the hot blotches of red on her cheeks, and felt a sudden, desperate desire for them to be in this together. To be able to mutter *"It's happening again, T,"* and have her know exactly what to say to make it better. She'd roll her eyes and squeeze his hand, say good-naturedly, *"At least the frog just sings. What happens when there's a full moon and that wolf wakes up?"*

Instead, Ray scooted back in his seat to sit on his hands, his fingers searching beneath him as if maybe they'd find a mouth for him to clap his hand over.

"If you refuse me, honey you'll lose me, then you'll be left alone..."

"Hey, asshole," said someone behind him. Ray turned to see a guy one row back leaning forward. "You wanna turn off your phone's stupid fuckin' ringtone?"

Ray considered his options for a moment, then decided that total denial was really his only choice. "My phone's on silent, dude," he said, turning back to the movie.

"Oh baby, telephone and tell me I'm your owwwwn."

"Then turn your *ass* off, moron," the guy said, and kicked the back of Ray's seat.

If only it were that simple, Ray thought to himself mirthlessly, as his wife stood up and walked out of the theater, and his frog launched into another jovial round of music.

*

There was only one tattoo Ray regretted wholeheartedly, and it was his own first name, written in medieval lettering along the side of his neck, thick and idiotic. It was borne of misguided pride and a lot of Jack Daniels, inked during his first year in the service and immediately deemed a "birth control tattoo" by his fellow Marines.

It makes you look fucking braindead, dude, his roommate had told him, examining Ray's neck and shaking his head. The edges of the tattoo were rough and the fill was a mottled, soupy gray like the sky before a storm. *I'm all for ink, but damn. It's not even centered. And does anyone even call you Raymond?*

That one started to twitch during a team meeting at work on a Monday morning. Ray had come to recognize the gentle tickle in his skin signaling that the antics were about to begin, like a feather brushing against him. He slapped a hand to his throat, trying to stifle it the way he would a sneeze. But it was too late—his neck tattoo was awake and ready to introduce itself.

The team lead was mid-presentation when it happened.

"I'M RAYMOND," the tattoo announced, so thunderously enthusiastic that everyone in the room swiveled toward Ray at the same moment, as if their heads were swinging on a single axis.

There was a round of uncertain laughter. Ray cleared his throat, put up a hand in apology. "I just… sorry, wasn't sure if we wanted to do introductions," he said, nonsensically, as they'd all been working on a long-term construction project together for the better part of a year. "Probably not. Carry on, John."

Looking puzzled, John returned to his presentation. Ray's neck throbbed, and he gritted his teeth and prayed the single outburst would be the end of it. He tried to catch someone's, anyone's, eye around the conference table—he'd begun to notice that his body seemed to misbehave only when no one was looking, like a child making faces behind a teacher's back.

He'd made this discovery on his way to work the week before; riding on a packed train, the "Semper Fidelis" tattoo on his inner arm started to tingle and pulse. He stared down at it, trying to catch a glimpse of it beginning to animate. Would the letters yawn open around a single mouth, or would small slits rip like loose seams? Would it ripple with sound? He examined the tattoo's smooth edges, still a crisp black—he'd gotten this one at a reputable spot in DC with some other guys in his platoon—but nothing happened. The words remained inert under his gaze, until finally he looked away, waiting for the sensation in his arm to recede as he stared out at the dark of the train tunnel. Only then did the sounds come.

The tattoo's first announcement was assertive but polite: *Semper Fidelis!* it declared at a perfectly reasonable volume, to which a man standing several feet away called back, *Hooah!* Encouraged, the tattoo grew louder: *SEMPER FIDELIS!*

Ray glared down at his arm, but the words were lifeless, soundless beneath his gaze, a row of sealed lips. The woman standing next to him scooted further away, and Ray glanced up in time to see her roll her eyes at the guy beside her.

SEMPER FIDELIS! the tattoo insisted the moment Ray looked away. *SEMPER FIDELIS!*

We get it, the guy muttered, and the woman said, *I don't even know what that means.*

Sorry, Ray said. Then he and the woman locked eyes for just a moment, and Ray felt that overwhelming pull again, the need for someone to understand what was happening to him. He wanted to tell this annoyed stranger everything: that he wasn't actually crazy or obnoxious, that his body was no longer his own, that it was betraying him—framing him! That this was not what he'd had in mind when he'd begun telling stories on his skin all those years ago. But then she turned away.

Semper Fidelis!

Jesus Christ, she said, then under her breath: *Freak.*

Sorry, said Ray.

Semper Fidelis, said the tattoo.

*

Three weeks in, Theresa told him that he needed to see a doctor.

They were sitting together on the bathroom floor, Theresa examining Ray's arm under the glow of her phone's flashlight.

"It's not infected, T," Ray mumbled as his wife examined the skull on his forearm, one hand covering her nose to block the stench of his skin. *This is just what a rotting skull smells like*, he thought darkly.

Theresa looked up at him, her face solemn. "Raymond. Are you kidding me right now? Your arm smells like a *literal* corpse." She shook her head. "I don't know why it doesn't look infected yet, but this is not good. Something is really wrong, Ray."

He nodded. "I know." He looked down at his wife, hunched over his arm, brows furrowed, so intent on fixing him. She hadn't changed out of her clothes from work and there was something comforting about the bright, sterile blue of her scrubs, the no-nonsense bun pinned to the nape of her neck. Her fingernails were cut short and her small hands looked delicate but capable: a nurse's hands, a mother's hands. "I think I'm losing it, Theresa," he whispered, though even as he said the words he knew they weren't quite right. What he meant was: *I'm lost.* Some tether had been loosened and now he was adrift, every direction wrong.

She looked at him, confused. To her, these were medical issues, plain and simple: infections with antidotes, problems with explanations and solutions. "You're okay, Ray," she said, gentle and reassuring. It was the voice she used to calm their daughter, the voice she probably used with her patients all day long.

"It's these fucking tattoos, T," he said. "I think I need to... I don't know. I think I need to get them removed or something."

It wasn't an option he'd ever considered before, and dread twisted in his gut the moment he said it. He'd always loved his tattoos, even the dumb ones. They were moments preserved in time, crystallized for display like an ancient insect caught in amber, and removal struck him as futile and misguided: an erasure of things that had already happened, a revision of solid facts. He liked what tattoos said about people—how each one offered a sliver of their history, a branch rising up from deep, hidden roots, promising plenty of tangle in the understory.

But maybe he'd had it all wrong. Maybe he should have kept his surface as solid earth, instead of trying to scrape legends into it. Maybe people didn't need a map of their lives splayed open for the world to decipher.

Theresa looked up from his arm, eyebrow raised. "Remove them? Okay, moneybags, right after you buy me that Porsche." She sat back on her heels and tucked a loose strand of hair behind her ear. "But an antibiotic might be more economical."

"I don't need an antibiotic, Theresa. I need it... I need them gone." He dropped his head into his hands, suddenly exhausted. "I just need all of them gone."

"Honey." Theresa leaned forward and pulled his hands away from his face. "Why don't you tell me what's really going on."

Ray looked down at his wife, so guileless, so certain she could help, and his body sagged beneath the weight of her certainty. What was there to do but come clean? He sighed, defeated.

"They've been coming alive." He shook his head to show that he knew he sounded psychotic, then continued. "The tattoos. One at a time. They take turns making my life a living hell." He held up his arm. "I guess this one can't come alive, so it... so it's dead. That's what the smell is. This dead fucking skull. And the scratches you saw on my back? The lion. Or maybe the wolf, I don't know. They both got me last week."

He kept his eyes averted as he spoke, afraid to see the look on his wife's face—afraid to see that wide openness slam shut. She had a handful of tattoos herself, but they were all cute, innocuous: three stars for her three sisters, a plump red heart on her ankle, a lunar moth spread open across her shoulder blades. Nothing that would piss off strangers or scare their daughter. Nothing that would ruin her life. Ray thought about what might happen if his wife's tattoos suddenly began to animate, imagined the shimmer of stars and the gentle throb of a heartbeat, the flutter of papery wings as the moth flitted across her skin in search of light.

There was a long silence before Theresa spoke. "Jesus *Christ*," she finally said.

Ray squeezed his hands into fists, wishing he'd kept his mouth shut. His wife was staunchly practical, so scientific in her view of the world that he sometimes worried their daughter was going to miss out on the magic of things. There was no talk of Santa Claus in their house, no promise of dollar bills and fairy dust under Poppy's pillow when she lost her first tooth. Theresa had no patience for that which couldn't be explained. When

Poppy was a baby, Ray had tried to talk his wife into just a few years of Santa visits—a handful of Christmas mornings before she started asking questions. *We don't even have a fireplace,* Theresa had said simply, as if their babbling one-year-old might push back against the logistics of Christmas lore.

Ray remained silent until finally Theresa spoke again. "Look, Ray," she said, and her voice had turned even, measured. "I'm not sure what's happening here. I don't know if this is about you getting older, or worrying about setting a bad example for our kid, or what."

Ray's heart sank. She thought he was crazy. Of course she did.

"I just don't know what to think," she went on. "What you're saying is... what you're saying is frankly batshit."

Ray nodded, ready to backtrack as much as she needed him to: *I wasn't being literal,* he'd say. *Obviously I was speaking metaphorically!* Or: *Gotcha! Totally kidding. You should see your face.* Then he would let her bandage his arm and drive him to urgent care and continue believing in a world built on tidy and rational explanations.

"But what I *do* know," she continued, "is that something really strange is happening to you. I've been trying to ignore it, but... the blood on your arm, the scratches, the sleep-talking—"

"The what?" Ray interrupted, confused.

"The sleep-talking," Theresa said. "Every night, the same shit over and over. Semper Fi, live free or die, that stupid Looney Toons song. One night you just kept yelling your own name. Sometimes you'd be snoring and talking at the same time, which really bugged me out. And now you come home smelling like a morgue and you tell me your tattoos are coming alive, and I… part of me wants to take you to the hospital or just fucking *commit* you or something, but… I don't know, Ray. The other part of me is like… maybe? Maybe what's going on with you is, like, exactly what you say it is?"

He blinked, unsure if he was understanding her correctly. He'd braced himself for every reaction except this one. She stared back, a wrinkle of concern between her brows.

"So… you believe me?" he asked finally. The words came out quiet, childlike.

Theresa shrugged. "I believe that your explanation is about as good as any. And man, that one night when you were snoring and talking… I swear your lips weren't even moving. It was some weird ventriloquism shit that I'm pretty sure you aren't actually capable of." She gave him a small, almost imperceptible smile, then said, "I'm also ninety-nine percent sure that snake on your leg flicked its tongue at me the other day."

Ray stared at her in disbelief before reaching out and wrapping his arms around her, pulling her to him so tightly that she let out a surprised laugh as she fell against his chest. "Thank you, T," he said into her hair. She smelled like flowers and soap and he breathed her in, feeling as if something had been loosened inside him, dislodged so air could flow freely again, so his heart could pump strong and steady.

She gave him a squeeze and then sat back to look at him. "So," she said, back to business. "The good news is, for whatever reason the stink of death seems to be going away." She reached for Ray's arm, held it aloft for them both to smell. She was right: the odor had all but vanished.

Ray gazed down at the small skull that rested along the seam of skin where his arm bent at the joint. The artist had used stippled shading around the skull's eyes and ears and along the crown of its head to create a look of decay, as if shreds of rotting skin still clung to the bones. *Sick*, Ray remembered saying when he saw the finished product, marveling at the vines that wormed their way into the skull's eye sockets, threaded through its nose and between the gaps in its sharp, crooked teeth. He looked back up at Theresa. "What's the bad news?"

She smiled ruefully and held her arms out at her sides as if to say, *Look around.* "The bad news is you're a medical anomaly, and short of spending Poppy's college fund on tattoo removal, I'm not sure what the hell we're supposed to do now."

Ray nodded, though he still felt so weak with relief at being believed, at sharing the burden of what was happening to him, that he hardly cared. His body tingled in a gentle, pleasant way, as if some subtle shift were happening beneath the surface of him, like stones in a riverbed rearranging beneath the weight of new water. Like maybe he could shed his layers to reveal new skin— still his own, still bearing all his stories, but calm, quiet. Skin that suspended beasts mid-roar and kept them caged, that offered sheepish glimpses into his past without also haunting his present, his future.

*

Ray lay beside his daughter in her bed, reading to her from the stack of books she'd presented to him at bedtime. She was cuddled up beside him, her little body warm and heavy with sleepiness, her dark curls still damp from her bath. They were on their sixth book of the night, but every time Ray stopped reading and began to climb out of her bed, Poppy's eyes would fly open and she'd beg him to continue. Theresa was good at putting a cap on the storytime routine, flipping off the light after book number four no matter how staggering the night's pile was, but Ray would read to Poppy until she was fast asleep and his own eyes had begun to droop shut.

Sucker, Theresa would chide him, but he knew she found it endearing, always telling people how he was wrapped around their daughter's finger, how all the clichés about girl dads were true. He knew there was pride nested in her teasing, that her eye rolls and snark belied a deep relief that this was the person he'd turned out to be.

He felt it too: relief that the tenderness of parenthood had come to him as easily as wildness had, that he could stay himself while also growing into someone else. That people could be a hundred different versions of themselves and have all of them be true—he could carve a prison tattoo into his best friend's skin in high school and still set a good example for his daughter, could cover his body in monsters and also chase them out from under her bed.

"This one, daddy," Poppy said, reaching over Ray to grab a collection of Grimm's Fairy Tales from the top of the pile. The book offered simpler, tamer versions of the original stories, accompanied by intricate illustrations that Poppy loved to examine. She'd run her little fingers over the drawings, tracing the branches of trees and the wings of fairies and narrating each picture as she went.

She walked her fingertips along Little Red Riding Hood's cape as Ray read, whispering to herself. "Pretty dress," she murmured, running a thumb along the hem as if she were feeling the fabric. "Scary wolf," she said, moving her fingers across the page to the Big Bad Wolf, who was lurking behind the trees. She traced a tiny fingernail along the tip of each fang. "Scary." She looked up at Ray. "Right?"

Ray shrugged. "A little scary, but just a book. Just a drawing, sweetie."

She nodded. "Just a drawing." She went to turn the page, then stopped "Do you like it, daddy?" she asked, pointing to the wolf again.

Ray paused, unsure how to answer her. He wondered if she was thinking about the wolf on his back, trying to reconcile its storybook villainy with everything she knew about her kind, silly daddy. "It's a nice drawing, don't you think?" he asked. "I like the drawing."

Poppy nodded. "It's good," she said, considering. "I don't want it though." She studied the drawing for a moment, then slid her finger back to Little Red Riding Hood. "I want her. I like her better because she's pretty and nice and brave." She nodded slowly, as if agreeing with herself. "You get the wolf and I get the princess," she announced. She'd gotten into the habit of referring to all female protagonists as princesses, and Ray bit back a smile.

"Okay," he said, smoothing the curls around her face.

She reached up and poked her finger into his cheek. "Riiiiight there."

"Right there what?" he asked, grabbing her finger and pretending to chomp down on it.

She giggled, pulling her hand away from him. "The drawing goes right there."

He feigned horror. "On my face?"

She nodded solemnly, then pointed to her belly. "And mine goes riiiiight here."

He laughed. "You want a drawing on your tummy?"

She shrugged, laying her head down on his chest. "Maybe." She yawned, readjusted herself against him.

Theresa poked her head into the room. She was wearing a bathrobe and her hair was knotted in a towel on top of her head. "Hey you two," she said, tying the sash of her robe around her waist. "I thought you'd be fast asleep by the time I got out of the shower." She crossed the room to give Poppy a kiss.

"We were having too much fun, weren't we, Pop?" Ray asked, smiling down at her.

Poppy nodded. "Daddy's getting a picture of the Big Bad Wolf and I'm getting Little Red Riding Hood. I'm getting it drawed on my tummy and he's getting it drawed on his *face*!" She patted Ray's cheek then collapsed into giggles.

Ray winked at his wife. "What do you think, T?"

Theresa sat down on the edge of the bed and tucked a stuffed bunny under Poppy's chin. "I think we can talk about it in about twenty years, Pop," she said, rubbing her back.

Poppy yawned, nuzzling deeper into the crook of Ray's arm, her round cheek so soft and new against his own storied skin. "What about daddy?" she asked, her voice thick with sleep.

Theresa turned to Ray. "Well, dad? Big Bad Wolf on your face at your four-year-old's request?" She smiled at him and their hands met along the curve of Poppy's back. She laced her fingers through his. "What do you say?"

"I say..." Ray smiled down at Poppy, at the tangle of her curls and at his wife's hands braided through his own, skin on skin on skin. "I say: someone grab me a pen and a sewing kit so we can get this party started."

FALLS

Alice lifts her dress above her knees and steps ahead of me, bare feet sinking beneath the surface of the water and then reappearing, slick and shimmering with silt. I unhook Maggie from her leash and she splashes into the water, paddling out past the rocks.

"Crazy thing," Alice says, knotting the hem of her dress at her thigh and wading further in. She'd shown up at my house that morning just as the sun was rising up from behind the trees, her arms loaded with grocery bags and Maggie's leash wrapped tight around her wrist.

"Should we walk to the river?" she'd asked, as if I'd been expecting her, and then headed toward the woods. We'd walked the trail in silence, our feet beating their familiar rhythm against the dirt, Alice behind me as I led the dog down the path.

I pull off my tennis shoes and follow her into the river, rolling my pants up as I go. The current weaves around my ankles, cold and rushing, too quick for the sun. In front of me Alice climbs over a rock to where Maggie is swimming, in the area where the water is deep and still below the waterfall.

"Fuck it's freezing," she says as she lowers herself in. The bottom half of her dress is wet now and clinging to her legs, sheer enough that I can see the pink of her skin beneath the flimsy blue.

"It's early," I say. "We always used to come in the afternoons."

She's standing waist-deep and I can see the rise of her belly beneath the loose folds of her sundress. She tucks her hands beneath her growing stomach, cradling its curve like there's already a baby in her arms. Then she closes her eyes and splashes backwards into the water, and for a moment the belly is all I can see, hard and buoyant like a separate creature. Maggie paddles over and pushes her snout against Alice's shoulder as Alice resurfaces, slicking her hair back with the palms of her hands. "You're not getting in?" she asks me.

I climb further up the wet rocks and look down at her. "It's cold. I'm tired." Drops of water are beaded along her eyelashes and she blinks them away.

"You didn't have to come." Her teeth are chattering but she makes no move to get out, her arms carving wide arcs in the water, keeping her afloat. "I just figured you'd want to see your dog."

I sit down and hang my legs over the edge of the rock, unrolling my pant legs to show that I have no plans to swim with her.

"Of course I wanted to see the dog."

It's been months since I've seen either of them. Maggie trots out of the water and settles in a patch of sunlight on the shore, her mouth hanging open in a sweet, dopey dog smile, happy and oblivious. We'd found her four years earlier, dirty and nearly starved to death in a cardboard box behind our house, so young her fur had felt slippery and matted in my hands. Together Alice and I had scrubbed her clean in the kitchen sink and then cooked her a hamburger that she ate carefully out of Alice's palm before falling asleep stretched across our laps. That first night Alice and I had stayed up late, smiling down at our new little creature, whispering our love for this shared thing as if we had created her ourselves.

"You should have called me. You just ran off with her." I'm surprised by the calmness in my voice, as if I'm launching some mild complaint. *You forgot to lock the front door. You left a clump of your hair in the shower drain. You moved out of our house with no explanation and took our dog with you. You got knocked up by somebody else and turned my life into a fucking joke.*

Alice shrugs. Her shoulders look narrow and bony, like a little girl's, and she reminds me of herself ten years ago. "I'm sorry. It all just seemed too hard."

"And this seemed like a better idea?" I wave a hand around, toward the bags of food sitting on the edge of the river and then up at the waterfall. "Disappearing for months and then bringing me here? To what, have a picnic? Go for a swim together? Do this stuff with your husband, Alice."

I expect her to get angry, but she just stares up at me.

"He's not my husband," she says, then kicks off the rocks and swims away.

We used to skinny-dip here together late at night, back when we first started dating, when everything was still a harmless adventure. We'd strip off our clothes and crash into the river, two streaks of white in the darkness, floating on our backs beneath the falling water, letting it batter our naked bodies for as long as we could bear it.

I stand up and cross back to where Maggie is stretched out in the sunlight. She lifts her head to look at me, then jumps up and starts sniffing around frantically, as if she's searching for a toy she's misplaced. I reach down and grab one of Alice's sandals. It's one she's had for ages, so worn through I can see the shape of her foot in the leather like a footprint pressed into the sand. I hold the sandal in my hand, run a thumb along the tiny crater of her pinky toe, then pitch it into the river. Maggie gallops in after it and I watch the sandal float along the surface of the water for a moment before it disappears beneath the current.

"What the hell, Ben?" Alice is climbing back toward the shore, holding her stomach as she steps gingerly from rock to rock. "Did you just throw my shoe in the river?"

I nod and pull a pack of cigarettes out of my back pocket. We'd been quitting together before she left, had even signed a long, earnest, drunken oath that we'd written while chain-smoking, as if we were eating our last meal before execution; smoking again after she was gone had felt like a delicious betrayal.

"I'm restoring order to the universe," I say, lighting a cigarette. "Your shoe was a sacrifice to the river gods."

"I've had those since college," she says.

Her dress is soaked through and I can see the familiar lines of her body beneath the fabric, almost naked but not quite, like I'm looking at her through someone else's glasses and the details are blurring together. I feel myself staring at her belly, at the foreign swell of it.

"I can't believe there's a baby in there," I say, which is sort of what I mean but not quite, and I realize I sound like a confused little kid pointing at his mother's pregnant stomach in awe. *A baby? In there?*

She crosses a hand over her body. "Ben..."

What I meant to say is: *I can't believe you're not just you anymore.*

She sits down beside me. "You're smoking again?" She takes the cigarette from me and examines it like she's looking for an answer. "To hell with vows at this point, I guess." She pinches the cigarette between her fingers, holds it up to her mouth like a threat. "Lucas would kill me," she says, and closes her lips around it. The cigarette dangles there, precarious, a choice waiting to be made.

I yank it out of her mouth and crush it into the sand. "What's wrong with you?" I ask, angry though I'm not sure why. "Jesus."

"What do you care?" She pulls her dress down over her knees as if she's suddenly self-conscious. I wonder if I should take off my shirt and wrap it around her, the way I would have in the past.

"I don't know," I say.

Her hair is starting to dry and the sun catches on a fleck of red. Her hair always lightens in the summer, auburn to dark strawberry, a tree turning early.

"I can't just all of a sudden not give a shit, Alice. I know it's none of my business, this baby, this guy, your husband or not-husband or whatever he is. But what am I supposed to do?"

She squints out at the river. The sun is bright above us now. "I wasn't actually going to smoke it," she says, pulling her legs up to her chest. "I'm not stupid. I just wanted to see what it would feel like to almost do it. Just to pretend things were different for a little while."

She twists her hair into a damp knot and looks over at me. I'm reminded of us here in this place a year ago, swimming together, handing shared cigarettes back and forth, falling asleep in the sun and then walking back to our house, sunburnt and tired. By then she was almost gone but I didn't know it; we'd been having long talks at night in bed, whispered arguments that never seemed to matter much in the morning. I didn't bother to worry because breakups only happened when people fought and shouted and cried, when they threw things at each other and broke dishes and threatened to leave a hundred times. Alice and I spoke quietly over one another, our voices overlapping and our words tinged with anger but both of us so calm and even that I didn't notice how treacherous things had become. She was trying to dig in roots while I tried desperately to pull them all up. *Let's go to Asia!* I'd say, like this was a logical answer to her questions about marriage and children. *Let's hike the Appalachian trail!* I ended up backpacking through the Rockies for a month without her, and when I came home she wasn't there anymore.

I pick up a small, gray stone and roll it between my fingers. *Philosopher's stones*, Alice used to say when she'd find ones that were smooth and flat and rested perfectly in the palm of her hand. *The kind that soothe you and give you answers.*

It's just a rock, you hippie, I'd tease, but the weight of certain stones always felt comforting and reminded me of her. I toss the stone into the river and Maggie perks up, watching it pierce the water's surface, then she looks back at me, her head cocked to the side as if to say: *Am I supposed to go in after it? I already know that it's gone.*

BLOOD LOSS

I wait for her at the blood bank on Chariot Street, and I know it's her as soon as she walks in the door. I've been in the waiting room for forty-five minutes, ushering people ahead of me each time a nurse calls my name, pretending to put the finishing touches on paperwork I finished ten minutes after I arrived. She hangs up her jacket and she's wearing pale green scrubs that hang loosely from her body. The slack neckline of her top slips down and I see a slice of white skin and the angle of her collarbone. Even under the folds of fabric I can tell that her body is slight and delicate. Her hair is pale blond, nearly white, and her face is muted, a blur of indistinct features, like a sketch of a woman that someone began and then set aside. There's something incomplete about her, and I wonder if this is what you wanted all along. This whisper of a person. This suggestion of something beautiful.

It occurs to me that she was probably with you this morning, that an hour ago the clothes she's wearing now were probably crumpled on your bedroom floor. I wonder if your smell is still on her skin.

I look down at the health forms in my hands, trace my pen along the curve of my name for the hundredth time, wait to hear the sound of her voice slam against me when she calls my name aloud.

Five minutes later she takes me into the back room, and I grip the forms so tightly that my fingernails punch through the paper and dig hard crescents into the palm of my hand. I don't know what I'm here to do. Yell at her, donate blood, slit her throat, cry like a child.

She gestures to a seat next to a man who is lying back in his chair, a bulging bag of blood beside him. He's reading a magazine like this is the most natural thing in the world, to let go of something that used to be a part of him.

"This shouldn't be too bad," she says to me. The skin on her face is thin and waxy, pulled taut across her bones as if it were made a size too small. She smiles, a reassuring smile that seems to inhabit her entire face, and wrinkles spring out around her eyes. I imagine the look on her face if suddenly I were to tell her who I am. I imagine sweeping an arm across her cart of needles and vials, smashing bottles under the heel of my boot, ripping the fat bags of anonymous blood from their tubes and bursting them against the walls. I picture the splatter of red against the bright, sterile white.

And then she rubs a swab of something cold across the stretch of my inner arm, murmurs that this won't take long at all, and for a moment I feel a sudden kind of tenderness toward her as her skin brushes mine. Her lips are dry and cracking, and a sliver of blood shines in the corner of her mouth. I search her vague, papery face for what might be extraordinary about her. She gives me a sympathetic look and I know she's misreading me, thinking I'm afraid of what she's about to do. She eases the needle into my arm and for a moment the thoughts are leached out of me and it feels like relief, like emptiness. The blood pushes and recedes and I can't think of anything else. And then I look up at her and the kindness of her smile slides back into focus, and the things she has taken from me feel more absent from my life than ever.

"It's amazing how much we can live without," the man to next to me says. His eyes are on the bag hanging beside me that's now growing plump with blood. I press my eyes shut but can feel the dull, throbbing rhythm in the crook of my arm where the needle is nestled inside me.

"We're more resilient than we think," she says. "After a little while your body will barely even register the loss." I open my eyes and she's leaning over me, holding the tube between her fragile fingers. They're small as a child's, but bony and frail in a way that betrays their age. The tube is nearly purple with the rush of blood.

When she walks away from me for a moment, I think about the things I'll say to her when she returns. I consider popping the tube out of my vein right then, leaving her to find my blood pooling, wasted, at her feet. I think of asking her what she has that I don't.

She comes back over and inspects the bag beside me, her small hands cradling it as though it's a living thing. She gives me a nod, as if to say, *We made it*, and reaches over to slip the needle out of me.

She presses a ball of cotton to my skin, like this is all it takes to heal me after she's pumped my insides out. She looks at me with the kind of removed sympathy that's reserved for strangers, for people who have no bearing on her actual life, and gives my shoulder a squeeze. "I'm sorry if that hurt," she says, and then with a wink, "but I think you'll survive."

She smoothes a bandage over my skin to seal it shut, leaving the fluff of cotton pressing up from underneath as though it's growing out of me, and tells me I did a great job, like I'm a child who's been extremely brave. And then she plucks the tube from the collection of my blood and rolls her cart away, shutting the door behind her, leaving me to survive on my own.

PROOF OF HAPPINESS

Her parents always said Michael was her first love. Next to Elizabeth at the dinner table he'd pluck coins from behind her ears, slide everything green from her plate to his own, jokingly tip his wine glass toward her smiling mouth. Her parents said she couldn't get enough of him. They said they knew she was a flirt even at six years old, watching the way she positioned herself to be tickled, leaned her weight against him when she was sleepy, hugged him long and hard every time he left the house. Her parents always seemed happy when he was there. They talked more when he was at the table, and the house felt like a different place in the hours when Michael came to visit. It took on a life that disappeared in his absence.

He married Kate when Elizabeth was eight, and Elizabeth adored her, wanted to imitate every move she made. She liked to sit between Kate and Michael on the couch, watching them watch each other, twirling their wedding rings between her fingers. They were always smiling. Her parents loved them too and they spent most weekend nights at Elizabeth's house, drinking beer and wine, spoiling her with presents, making her parents laugh, filling the quiet house with life.

When Kate got pregnant a few years later, Elizabeth was mesmerized and in love. She stroked Kate's wide, hard belly, whispered into Kate's skin so that the baby would know her voice. She asked if they would name it after her. Through the layers of Kate's shirt she would whisper to the baby that she loved it. Sometimes she thought about what it would be like if Kate and Michael adopted her. Sometimes she thought about marrying Michael. That was harder because she was in love with Kate too and wanted her around. She wanted to marry both of them. She wanted to be a part of their happiness.

Elizabeth held Danny the day they brought him home from the hospital, writhing and hot in his blue cotton blanket, his tiny red fingers clamped around her thumb with a strength that surprised her. He cried in her arms and nothing she did helped. His choked wails embarrassed her and she gave him back quickly; she'd wanted everyone to marvel at how naturally they took to each other. Later she visited him when he was napping in his crib, repeated "Mama" over and over again, hushed and gentle, the way she pictured a mother would speak to her baby. She didn't see Kate watching from the doorway.

"He won't be able to speak for a long time, Elizabeth," Kate said. She came in and lifted him to her, her hand pressed to the back of his head, his chubby legs curled over the crook of her arm. She unbuttoned the top of her shirt and Danny pushed his face along her freckled chest, his eyes still squeezed shut. "I'm gonna feed him now, sweetie. Why don't you go see your parents?" Her engagement ring sparkled in the dim light from the street lamps outside, and Elizabeth touched her finger to it, running her fingernail over the edges of its diamond.

She smiled up at Kate, pinched Danny's foot lightly. "I love you, Danny," she whispered. She wished Kate would let her stay while she fed him. "I love you, Kate." Kate looked tired and beautiful in the dark of the room. She and Michael were living in a house in Brooklyn Heights, and Danny's room was decorated in pale blues and greens, the outline of boats and buses and fire engines stenciled into the panels of the walls. He was named after Kate's dad.

Maybe next time, kid, Michael had told Elizabeth when they'd found out they were having a boy and seen the disappointment in her face. *Wouldn't be fair to name the poor guy Elizabeth, would it?* He'd said this with one hand pressed to Kate's growing stomach.

*

Elizabeth's parents divorced a year after Danny was born. She'd gotten used to the rise of their screaming voices in the next room and to the days of silence that always followed. She knew that her dad almost never slept in bed with her mom, knew that sometimes he didn't sleep in their house at all.

They'd stopped eating meals together, which was easier than watching her parents avoid each other's eyes, flinch if their fingers accidentally touched, slide past one another like strangers. Michael and Kate stopped bringing Danny over, and instead Elizabeth would visit them with one parent or the other. In the days after her parents told her about the divorce, Kate took Elizabeth out with her and Danny nearly every afternoon, to the park and the library, grocery shopping, to the laundromat. Kate thought she was sad and so Elizabeth let her believe that, never admitting that it was easier this way, that she never thought her parents liked her or each other much anyway. She'd never seen her dad touch her mom the way Michael touched Kate; her mom never kissed her forehead the way Kate kissed Danny's. No one in Elizabeth's house ever said *I love you.*

*

Sophomore year of high school, Elizabeth got caught drinking. Her dad had just remarried, to a woman named Camille who stacked bottles of wine and whiskey in the cabinets and smoked at the dinner table, her cigarette aimed toward the doorway as if that made a difference. When she spoke, tufts of smoke popped from her lips and she waved the clouds away with her hand as if dismissing her own words.

One night when she and Elizabeth's father were out at a party, Elizabeth and her friends emptied the cabinets of Camille's alcohol, pouring tumblers of whiskey and refilling the bottles with water until the remaining liquid was nothing but a pale caramel, a shade away from clear. They got drunk and loud and careless, carrying their glasses out onto the front stoop, smoking cigarettes and flicking the butts onto the neighbor's adjoining porch.

Elizabeth had been babysitting Danny for nearly two years by then; he was four and they adored each other. Three days a week she caught the subway out to Brooklyn Heights and stayed with him while Kate ran errands, and they played together as if they were best friends, brother and sister, mother and son. She rolled on the floor with him, spoke to him in secret languages, loved him as fiercely as she could imagine loving someone.

After the divorce, her parents had started seeing Michael and Kate less and less, the friendship another casualty of their marriage's collapse. But babysitting Danny had kept Elizabeth a part of Michael and Kate's life, and she was with them several nights a week, on her own, a member of their family. Her life with them had nothing to do with her parents, or with anyone else. She was a different person when she was with them. Sometimes her parents told her she was intruding, that Michael and Kate needed time on their own, but Elizabeth believed that her place in their lives was something her parents couldn't understand. Their family was everything hers couldn't be. They were proof that happiness was possible.

Her dad caught her drunk that night after her friends had all stumbled home. One of the neighbors had called him, complaining that Elizabeth and her friends had been yelling obscenities, that a bottle had been smashed on the front steps, that a boy had peed in a flower pot. Elizabeth had laughed at that, a beer still in her hand, one of Camille's cigarettes pinched between her fingers.

"It was just a little party," she told him. "Now there's less for Camille to drink, so that's good." She'd stopped caring what her father thought of her. She'd stopped thinking of him as more than a man whose house she shared two days a week and every other weekend.

"Don't think you're getting away with this, Elizabeth," her dad said, ripping the beer can from her hand and slamming it into the kitchen sink. He took the cigarette from her lips and stabbed it out. He'd grown old somehow, the skin around his eyes lined and sagging, his hair thin wisps of silvery brown. Elizabeth couldn't believe that he and Michael had ever been friends—Michael with his laughing eyes and blond, grayless beard, beautiful wife and perfect child. It seemed impossible to Elizabeth that her old, sad parents were the ones who had brought these people to her.

The next day her father told Michael what had happened, told him she'd made "quite the display," thanks to her worthless friends and the better part of a bottle of Maker's. He said all of this while Elizabeth sat beside him, pawing for the phone, demanding to speak to Michael and Kate herself. Later that night they called back, said they'd spoken about it for a long time and had decided it would be better if she not take care of Danny for a while.

"You can still come over sometimes," Michael told her. "I just don't know that this is a good time for you to have a lot of responsibility. You're great with Danny, Liz, but I'm not sure we can rely on you right now. Just while you're going through this phase."

She begged him not to take Danny from her, cried into the phone until her dad came into the room and told her she was being ridiculous.

"I love you," she whispered into the phone. "I love you all, all three of you."

Michael coughed and told her to calm down, that she was acting like this was a death sentence.

"You're the only people I love," she told him. Then her dad picked up the line in the hallway and told her to stop acting hysterical.

"I'm sorry, Mike," he said. "I don't know what's gotten

into her. She's fine though. Hang up the phone, Elizabeth, it's time to say goodnight."

After school the next afternoon, she got on the subway from Park Slope and headed to Brooklyn Heights the way she always did on Mondays. She clutched a copy of *The Nightgown of the Sullen Moon* in her hands, a gift from Michael and Kate from years before. She wanted to read it to Danny, wanted to remind Michael and Kate that she was part of their family, that they'd all loved each other since she was a child. She looked down at the inscription on the first page, written in Kate's loose, sweeping cursive: *A favorite to be read again and again, for our dear Elizabeth. Love, Michael and Kate.* Love. She let her eyes rest comfortably on the word, felt the weight of it in her limbs while the train knocked along toward Michael and Kate's safe, beautiful house.

Kate was sitting on the front porch when Elizabeth got there, rocking Danny in her arms awkwardly, his long limbs sprouting in all directions, the front of her shirt streaked with tears. For a moment Elizabeth felt satisfied, imagined Danny crying at the front door, waiting for her. Bursting into tears when Kate said Elizabeth wasn't allowed to come over anymore, throwing himself to the ground inconsolably.

"Elizabeth," Kate said, squinting at her across the front lawn. "What are you doing here?" She patted Danny's back gently, her long fingers curling through a tuft of his pale hair. "Dan had a bit of a fall. Got a little too daring on that scooter."

Elizabeth crossed over to the porch and sat down on the steps beside them, stroked one of Danny's legs, soft with blond fuzz like a sweet little peach. He wiped a hand across his wet face and smiled at her, his cheek pressed tight against Kate's neck.

"I'll take him," Elizabeth said, reaching into Kate's arms.

Kate pulled back, looked straight at her. Kate's eyes were bright green, the kind of eyes Elizabeth had always wanted, rimmed in a chocolatey brown, fading to a color like celery at the pupils. "I can't have you over here so much anymore, hon," Kate said, sitting Danny up straight on her lap. He squirmed out of her grasp and ran down the steps and back to his overturned scooter. Kate's voice was kind but stern, a voice Elizabeth had heard her use with Danny when he got into trouble. Elizabeth's mother had never perfected that voice: she was too meek, too unsure of herself as a mother to ever convince Elizabeth she meant business. Elizabeth scared her more than she scared Elizabeth.

"But I want to help." A thread was coming loose at the hem of Kate's shirt and Elizabeth reached for it, wrapped it tight around her pinky, trying to rip it free. She could feel Kate watching her.

Kate pulled the thread away, brought it to her lips and snipped it loose with her front teeth. "I know you do. But you're getting into trouble, you're not spending any time with your parents." She sighed and crossed her hands in her lap. Her nails were painted light pink, almost the color of her skin. "You should be with your own family."

Elizabeth asked if she could stay for dinner and Kate said they had people coming over, but maybe sometime next week. She asked if she could play with Danny for a while, and Kate just sighed. "How would that be any different than always?" she asked, getting to her feet.

"Elizabeth." Her voice was coarse. "We all need some space from you. I'm sorry, but we do." She started picking things up from the yard, filling a wide red bucket with Danny's toys. "It has nothing to do with you. But we're a family, and we need some time on our own. And so do you. You need some time to figure things out." She took Danny's hand and led him up the front steps. He stopped midway and wrapped his arms around Elizabeth, leaning into her lap, his hands knotted through her hair.

"Lizzy, Lizzy, Lizzy," he sang. His cheek was pressed to hers and she wanted to squeeze him until neither of them could breathe. She wanted to make him cry just so she could comfort him, so she could wipe the tears from his soft face and press his small, sturdy frame to hers, feel how much he loved her in his little hands laced through her fingers, his warm breath in her ear.

She ran into Michael on her way to the subway. He was wearing a suit, his tie loosened around his neck. She fell against him when she saw him, pushed her face against his chest until he stumbled backward.

"Hey now," he said, his hands on her shoulders. "It can't be that bad."

She cried against him, leaning back into his hand when he lay it gently on her head, running her head along his palm so that his fingers stroked her hair. He pulled back, but she held the edges of his suitjacket in her fists and stared up at him, her eyes clouded with tears. Then she pushed her lips against his neck and breathed in the salt of his skin, sweaty from a day in the city. She could smell the faintness of his aftershave, a smell that she thought of as being only his. Her father never wore aftershave, or if he did she was never close enough to him to smell it. Michael smelled like what a man, a husband, a father, needed to smell like. His skin tasted familiar, pressed to her lips, as if she'd always known what it would be like.

He stepped away from her, holding her at arm's length. "Buck up, kiddo," he told her. "It's not the end of the world." He unhooked her fingers from the buttonholes of his jacket. Then he kept walking, away from her.

She didn't babysit at all after that. Kate got a nanny and went back to work; Michael invited her over for occasional dinners, and he and Kate started treating Elizabeth like a guest, taking her coat when she arrived, seating her in the living room while Kate cooked in the kitchen. Elizabeth used to help with dinner, her hands instinctively knowing where Kate kept the serving dishes, how many dashes of oregano she liked to put in the pasta sauce. Now when Danny would play at Elizabeth's feet or pull at her arms to follow him down to the playroom, Michael would tell him not to bother her. He'd ask about her parents, tell her about work, make chitchat as if she were an acquaintance who'd just happened to drop by.

Somehow it seemed impossible to Elizabeth that they could continue to act like a family in her absence. At dinner, when Michael and Kate would joke about something she hadn't been around for, when they'd talk about someone she'd never heard of, Elizabeth would look back and forth between them, waiting to be filled in, waiting for them to prove she hadn't been removed from their family. She gave them opportunities to tell her how much they missed her. "With school letting out in a few weeks, I don't know what I'm gonna do with myself," she'd say, letting the words hang in the air, waiting for Michael and Kate to offer themselves to her. Sometimes she talked about how her mother was never around, twisting the words so it sounded like she cared, like she wanted her mother there. Like she needed someone to fill that place. They just nodded and listened, frowned when her stories demanded a frown, looked down at their plates when she hinted at what she wanted from them. Sometimes the table would grow quiet and Elizabeth would want to scream just to fill the space. It reminded her of dinners with her parents all those years ago, dinners with nothing but clinking forks, grinding teeth, the air tight with things unsaid. It wasn't supposed to be like that with Michael and Kate and Danny; they were supposed to be a family who shouted *I love yous* through the hallways. Who wrapped their arms around each other for no reason but because it felt good, proved their love in a million different ways, knew the feel of each other's hands on their skin the way they knew the contours of their own faces.

A week after Elizabeth turned seventeen, Michael and Kate had a housewarming party at their new home in Flatbush. It was a big, welcoming house, with a wide porch that wrapped around to the backyard and an attic that had been converted into Danny's bedroom.

It was Elizabeth's first time at the house, and it had already been filled with all their furniture, its walls covered with the paintings and photographs she knew so well. Everything seemed out of place in this beautiful new house. Everything looked foreign to her. She hated the fresh blond wood of the steps, the brass knocker on the front door, the smell of new paint, strangers' perfumes, food cooking in a kitchen she'd never seen. She brought her boyfriend with her, a college freshman named Brad who she'd been dating for about four months. He was nice enough, a quiet guy with floppy hair and long, skinny legs. It was Elizabeth's senior year of high school and the first year guys had started paying any attention to her at all. She'd let her hair grow down past her shoulders and learned how to twist it into thick waves, how to apply winged eyeliner and the right lipstick, and that seemed to make all the difference. She wore tighter clothes, cultivated a sultry apathy they seemed to find sexy, and by Christmas she had a boyfriend.

Elizabeth left Brad at the refreshment table in the living room and wove her way through the crowds of unfamiliar faces. She didn't know any of them and wondered how they all knew Michael and Kate. Everyone was laughing and chatting, cupping hors d'oeuvres in their palms, holding glasses of wine and flutes of champagne. She grabbed some champagne from a table in the corner and headed down the hallway. She found Kate in the kitchen, an apron wrapped around her hips, her light hair trimmed short. Elizabeth hadn't seen Kate in nearly eight months; Kate and Michael had stopped inviting her over, had taken to waiting a week or two before returning her calls. When she talked to them about it they laughed it off, said they were busy, said she should drop by when things were less hectic. Elizabeth hadn't even known they were leaving Brooklyn Heights until the invitation to their party arrived in the mail.

Kate came around the kitchen table to hug Elizabeth, wiping her floury hands down the front of her apron. She smelled the way she always had, like flowery shampoo and the light chemical scent of department store perfume. Elizabeth had tried the perfume on before, dabbed it behind her ears, rubbed it between her wrists the way Kate always did, but on Elizabeth it smelled silly, made her think of little girls with streaks of red lipstick across their faces and strings of pearls draped around their tiny bodies. It smelled like she was pretending to be grown up, playing at being a woman.

"You look beautiful," Kate said. She wound a piece of Elizabeth's long hair around her hand and Elizabeth leaned gratefully into Kate's arms, let out a breath she hadn't realized she'd been holding. She wanted Kate to whisper into her hair how much she loved her, how much she missed her. She wanted to be held there forever, locked in Kate's arms, as safe as a child in the arms of her mother.

But Kate let go quickly, and then they were separate again, the voices of strangers invading the space between them, reminding Kate that she had shrimp to cook, a cake to ice. She told Elizabeth that Danny was in the backyard and Michael was out buying another case of wine. She glanced at the champagne in Elizabeth's hand. "I guess it's not really my place to tell you not to drink that," she said, smiling. "Just take it easy, sweetheart."

Elizabeth and Brad stayed at the party for hours. They drank too much and danced together in the center of the living room, their hips pressed together, their hair sweaty and sticking to their faces. Michael was drunk too, laughing and hooting as she and Brad thrashed to the music. He and some friends from work got up and joined them, and together they all writhed to the loud throb of Johnny Cash with the bass too high. Kate didn't say anything, just passed in and out of the living room, rolling her eyes, turning down the music only to have one of them reach over and turn it back up. A part of Elizabeth knew she was making things worse, that in the morning Michael and Kate wouldn't think anything of her except that they'd been right all along, that she didn't deserve to be in their lives, that Danny was better off not knowing her at all. But she let the alcohol course through her, sway her body with the pulsing music, and through a haze of champagne she felt her boyfriend grind his body against her while she watched Michael laugh and dance just a few feet away. She reached her hand, slick with sweat, out toward Michael and he gripped it in his, his eyes smiling, unsuspecting, drunk with love for anything and everything. Elizabeth slid her hips away from Brad's body so that they were angled toward Michael and ran a hand through the tangle of her hair. She knew men liked her hair this way. She knew they liked her body. She rocked her hips closer to him, parting the crowd of his friends with her swaying limbs. He reached toward her and playfully tugged a piece of her hair. The song ended and he turned away, raising a beer to his lips. "I bet that one woke Danny up."

"Damn right it did," Kate said. She was clearing off the coffee table, a jumble of glasses and plates tucked under her arm. "Go up and check on him, Mike. For Christ's sake." She didn't look at Elizabeth as she brushed past. Elizabeth took a last sip of champagne and followed Michael toward the staircase.

"I hope he's awake so I can say goodnight," she said as they climbed the stairs. "He was so distracted with the other kids I hardly got to see him at all."

"He was glad to see you, Liz," Michael said. "He's always glad to see you." He handed her his beer and she took a long sip.

"You must be drunk, giving me your beer to drink."

Michael shrugged. "I'm not your father, Elizabeth, and you're almost a grown-up now." He rounded the second flight of stairs and took the beer from her, swigging the last of it. "I'm not here to discipline you."

"You mean you don't care anymore." Her toe caught on the top step of the staircase and Michael reached out to catch her elbow. She held tight to his arm as they made their way to the attic stairs.

"Of course I care. It's just different now, kid." He shrugged. "You've got a life, we've got a life. That's the way it's supposed to be."

"But I want to be a part of your life." She could feel the alcohol buzzing in her head, pulsing like a heartbeat behind her eyes. She sat down at the foot of the attic stairs and held her head in her hands. Michael crouched down in front of her, his hands resting on her knees.

"Need some water? Man, I shouldn't have bought so much alcohol for this damn party." He lifted her chin with his forefinger and swept a clump of sweaty hair out of her eyes. She pushed her face into the hollow between his neck and shoulder, felt his sweat sticky against her. He kissed the top of her head and she gripped his shoulders.

"Why don't you love me?" she demanded suddenly. She looked him hard in the eyes. "You love Kate. You love Danny. Why not me?" Her face was wet with sweat and tears, and she pushed herself against his parted mouth. His teeth grazed her cheek and she pulled him against her, her back slamming hard against the stairs.

"Stop it. Jesus." He tried to pull away from her but she held tight, her hands clamped behind his neck.

"Just say you love me. You're the only people I've ever loved, and you hate me now."

"You're acting crazy, Elizabeth. No one hates you." His eyes were unfocused, glazed with alcohol and confusion, and she could smell the heavy coating of champagne and beer on his breath. She reached her mouth toward his, tasted the bite of salt and the bitterness of liquor on his lips and tongue. She squeezed him against her but couldn't get him close enough. She lay back on the steps and for a moment he leaned with her, on top of her, their bodies falling into each other. The weight of him on her felt like relief, like love, and their mouths stayed pressed together, suspended and unmoving, their teeth grating against each other. They weren't kissing, but rather breathing into one another, heaving hot breath back and forth between their parted mouths. And then he was standing. He was straightening his clothes. He was rubbing his fists deep into his eyes.

"I'm sorry," Elizabeth whispered.

He shook his head.

"I'm sorry," she said again. "I just wanted..." She squeezed her eyes shut, listened to the dim buzz in her mind, watched the muted black behind her eyelids.

And then she stood and headed for the stairs that led her out of this beautiful, unfamiliar house. This house she would never be at home in, that would never welcome her the way she needed to be welcomed. She turned back to Michael, resting her hand on the railing: gleaming new wood just waiting for this perfect family to wear it away with their hands, to scratch it and scuff it and give it a life.

REFUGE

There's a stretch of road off the highway that she drives with her eyes pressed shut. It's a dirt road out to Zach's house, a straight shot just wide enough for two cars to slide past each other if they stay steady, if neither veers even a bit. Hardly anyone drives this road and in the late night black she slams her foot hard on the gas and imagines there is real danger in what she's doing. She pictures opening her eyes to the screech of tires, her side mirror crashing though a passing car's window, the flank of the car spiraling her off into the surrounding marshes. She imagines the nose of her car bouncing and sloshing down into the water, the headlights braiding through the yellowing marsh grass, her eyes wide open. She imagines Zach finding her. She imagines people asking him what she'd been doing on the road to his house in the middle of the night.

The house is quiet and she can see Zach stir as she lets herself in the back door. He's shirtless on the couch, his jeans caked with dirt. His arms are folded over his chest and his hands are gripped around his shoulders, so tightly that she expects to see the indent of his fingernails pushed into his skin as she coaxes him awake. He opens his eyes for a moment, asks her what time it is, tells her that the nurse is coming early so she can't stay the night. She sits on the edge of the couch, her leg grazing his. She slides her hand across his chest for a moment then pulls it back into her lap.

"Annie had a good day," he says, even though this means nothing. Meg nods. Zach judges his wife's days by his own, telling people she seems healthy on days when work is easy or the Braves win a game, saying that she looks sad and pale on the days when the most he can manage is sitting wordlessly in the corner of her room.

He slides a cold hand beneath the hem of Meg's dress and she stretches herself across him. His arms fold limply around her and they both keep their eyes sealed shut.

*

It started a year ago, the day of Aaron's funeral—before anyone was sure Annie would survive, before Meg was out of her cast and before the slashes on her arms and legs had stopped bleeding for good. She was out in the backyard, coatless, in a black dress and bare feet, one of Aaron's sweaters draped over her arm. She liked the feel of the cold on her naked shoulders, the remnants of frost poking up between her toes on blades of uncut grass.

She and Zach hadn't spoken in the days after the accident. He'd been released from the hospital almost immediately, the only one of the four of them to have come out mostly unscathed, a miraculous injustice. The driver was supposed to die. The driver wasn't supposed to climb his way out of the ruins while her husband lay pinned beneath wreckage he hadn't created. She blamed

Zach, hated him fiercely until he was standing in front of her in the backyard that day, hours after Aaron's funeral. And then her hands were on his face, pressed to the bandage strapped across his nose, tracing the gash through his eyebrow. She pushed her fingertips against the thin skin of his eyelids, the way mothers coax children into sleep, the way doctors put the wide-eyed dead to rest. He closed his eyes willingly and fell hard into her. "You need a coat," he said into her forehead, his mouth hot on her skin.

"No, this feels good." The words seemed so ridiculous, so impossible. She tried them again. "This feels good," she said, and pulled away. She was a wife at her husband's funeral. "This feels good."

Zach opened his coat and pulled her inside, wrapping it tight around her. They were standing over the grave of Aaron's cocker spaniel, an oval of dirt where the grass had been scraped away. Two wooden stakes were nailed into a cross and stabbed into the ground; Meg could remember Aaron taking her out here when she'd first started dating him, telling her about his childhood pet with such reverence that at first she'd thought he was joking. She'd made fun of him to her friends afterward, telling them he was too sensitive for her, but she'd begun to secretly love him a little that day.

Meg led Zach wordlessly down the outdoor staircase into the cellar of her husband's parents' house, glared up into his swollen eyes until his mouth was on hers. Their faces were wet against each other even though she hadn't seen him cry, hadn't felt herself cry. And then, pressed against a cement wall, gripping naked pipes, they yanked their clothes aside and pushed blindly into one another. He slammed her into the splintered wood of the staircase and she wrapped her legs around him, close to laughter. At one point she cried out; he clapped a hand over her mouth and she bit hard into him. Afterwards, she saw that the stitches in her knee had broken open and slathered her leg in blood.

*

She hates going into Annie's room now. Zach keeps the blinds wide open, says the light helps, says that Annie loves to be able to see the ocean. But Meg usually sees the room in blackness, when the only light flickers from monitors and shines out over the shape of Annie beneath the blankets. Annie never speaks, never looks at Zach or Meg or the nurses who come to see her, just stares at her hands, her eyes watery and unfocused. Some nights Meg will look in and see Zach angling Annie's face toward his, pressing his lips to the colorless skin of her cheek while her eyes fix on something in the distance. Sometimes Meg forgets that Annie is still his wife. She forgets that she and Zach are not grieving the loss of their lovers together, because to Zach the sight of Annie's breathing body, the rise of her chest and whistle of her breath, are refuge enough from grief. But Meg remembers Zach and Annie as a couple the way she remembers Aaron as her husband; the husk of Annie is only as real to her as the space beside her in bed, the memory of her husband's hands on her skin, the raised earth of his grave.

Zach keeps pictures all around Annie's bed, of him and her together: their wedding, their honeymoon, their high school prom. They'd shared a limo with Meg and Aaron and in an album somewhere there was a prom picture of the four of them together. A month after graduation Meg had been Annie's maid of honor, and a few years later Annie was Meg's. Once they'd talked about what they thought of each other's husbands, laughing, scrunching up their noses, promising each other it was too weird even to joke about.

"I can't even think of Aaron as having *anatomy*," Annie had said, burying her face in a pillow. "He's like my brother." She'd laughed and smacked the pillow across Meg's lap. "Not that he isn't adorable, of course."

But although Meg had feigned disgust at the thought of Zach as a husband, nodding and agreeing that he too was like a brother to her, even in high school she'd loved him in a quiet way. She'd wanted to marry Aaron, she wouldn't have chosen anyone over him, but there had always been a thrill in Zach's mere proximity. He'd adored her because she was his best friend's girlfriend and then his best friend's wife, but there had been times when she'd wished she could step out of her life with Aaron just for a moment. Sometimes when she and Zach lay together now, their bare bodies pressed together the way she never thought they could be, she thought of telling him, of saying she'd always wanted this, but the words playing over in her mind sounded like betrayal. She wasn't even sure who it was she was betraying.

*

Meg can see the first shafts of sunlight through the living room window and Zach is no longer beside her on the couch. He's covered her in a blanket and she knows that he probably left her down here hours ago. She wraps the blanket around herself and heads upstairs. The house is quiet except for the creak of her feet against the cold wood of the floors and the faint ticking of Annie's monitors.

At the top of the stairs, she turns to stand in the doorway of Annie's room; Annie is sitting upright, her eyes open, and beside her Zach is curled around her body, his head resting against her stomach, his hand gripped around hers. He has a room of his own, what used to be the guest room, but in the early mornings this is where Meg usually finds him. When he lets her spend the night they sleep in the guest room, tucked away from the rest of the house, though Meg still sees his eyes dart constantly toward the doorway. It's as if some part of him believes Annie could awaken from this half-sleep and find them there, squeezed together in that old twin bed, having sex with a pillow stuffed between the wall and the headboard to mask the sound, like teenagers in their parents' house.

Zach opens his eyes and pushes closer to Annie, then notices Meg in the doorway. "You heading out?" he asks, running a hand through the mess of his hair. His other hand still holds tightly to Annie's.

She shrugs. "I don't have work till ten," she tells him, moving further into the room. She stops at the foot of the bed. She never gets too close to Annie, never touches her anymore.

The vacancy in Annie's eyes is searing. Sometimes she wonders if Annie is listening to what's going on, if everyone is wrong and she's aware of it all, if she's just building up the strength to claim back her husband.

"Well, the nurses will be here soon, so you probably shouldn't stay too long."

Meg can see the sun rising just over the outline of Spanish oaks outside, leaking a muted orange light through the heavy branches. She knows Zach can't stand the idea of the nurses seeing her here, of them thinking he's surrendered the idea that Annie may recover, that he's found someone new.

"Come lie with me in the other room for a while," Meg says, even though she knows he won't. He doesn't look at her.

"I just want to be here," he says. His face is inches from Annie's and he says this into her hair. "I just want you to go and I want to be here."

Meg takes another step closer, smells the quiet odor of sweat and dirt on Annie, veiled by the scent of soaps scrubbed carelessly over her skin by nurses. "She's not alive," Meg tells him, even though she knows it does nothing when she says these things.

"Of course she is." Zach lays his hand across Annie's chest and pushes his face against the hollow of her cheek. "Her heartbeat is stronger than mine." He moves her hand to his chest but it falls to the side. He looks up at Meg. "I'm sorry," he says. "I'm sorry, I don't know why you bother with me."

Meg crosses to him and brushes a hand through his hair. It's damp and sticky with grease, and she pushes it away from his eyes. He puts a finger to her lips and she takes it between her teeth, bites slowly down until he cringes and pulls away. She wants him to bite back, to run his fingers through her hair too, and then yank until she can't think, to pull her to the floor and disappear into her. But he just watches her sadly, and she knows that all he wants is for her to leave. He wants the relief of the front door slamming behind her, of her car crunching away down the drive until he can be alone, with Annie.

*

On her way back toward the highway, Meg sees a car coming toward her. It's in the middle of the narrow dirt road, probably the first morning nurse. Meg drives steadily toward it, her eyes open, her hands tight on the wheel. But as they near each other she slips off to the right as the oncoming car moves to her left, and they glide easily past. She has trouble imagining crashing into the marshes in the daylight; when she thinks of a crash, she pictures headlights slicing wildly through darkness, fire exploding from the hood into the black, screams coming from places she can't see. She pictures her husband's chest pinned beneath stretches of metal, and flames erupting around his bleeding legs. She pictures Zach sliding out from beneath the wheel, pulling at her arms, leaning his weight against the belly of the overturned car. She can see Annie motionless in the dirt, all thought and memory slammed out of her, blood snaking down her face thick and black. She remembers Annie being taken away separately, while Aaron was pulled from the car, his eyes pressed shut by bloody hands and his face covered over before he was even put in an ambulance. And then she and Zach were carried away, hurt only on the surface, taken to hospital corridors where people breathed freely, where they recovered, where they were stitched up and expected to go on living.

WITH HER

There are still moments when the scent of her makes me worry that she has ruined me for other women. Once, months ago, I watched her dance by herself, her white fingers pinching the fabric of her dress so that it swung lazily around her ankles, and I felt as if I could breathe in her smell from across the crowded dance floor.

She likes to cook me dinner even now, even though I have a life entirely separate from her, even though our reason for knowing each other is gone. When I see her she still holds onto me tight, cradles my face against the softness of her neck. My father left her years ago, the same way he left my mother at the start of my life, but when she holds my face in her hands I know she sees a son, a person to love even though my father is gone. She likes to cook me elaborate meals, but always pretends that she'd been planning to prepare them all along. "I have some extra chicken over here, if you want to help me out," she'll say into the phone, and I can picture her standing in the doorway of the kitchen, an apron draped over her narrow hips. I always go, even though she lives on the other side of the city and it sometimes takes me an hour each way. My girlfriend doesn't understand, thinks it's strange for me to continue to visit a stepmother who was divorced from my father by the time I was fifteen years old.

"Diana is not your responsibility," Kim will tell me, as if I'm simply playing caretaker. I've been with her for three years now, and she's taken to speaking to me in that sharp, confident tone of voice that women only use when they're sure a man isn't going to leave them. "If she's so lonely why doesn't she just remarry? It's not like you're related to her."

I was introduced to Diana for the first time when I was ten years old. My father had spent the years following his split from my mother dating loud women who laughed raucous laughter and had no idea how to talk to me. The woman before Diana had long fingernails that she would rake up and down my father's thighs when we sat at the dinner table, whispering things to him while I watched them wordlessly; another one insisted that I flex my muscles every time she came over to the house. She would wrap her hands around my thin, hairless arm and shriek about how strong I was, then laugh in my father's face as if she'd said something remarkably clever.

Diana loved to dance. My father took her dancing the first time they went out, a shift from the noncommittal movie dates he usually treated women to, and I wonder if maybe he knew she was different right from the start. He brought her home to meet me that first night; I'd been curled up on the couch beside my sleeping babysitter, and my father had twirled Diana into the living room, both of them singing "Summertime" in hushed, laughing voices. Diana was tall and young, her gray eyes watery with giddiness and alcohol, and my father's suit jacket hung from her slender shoulders as if it belonged to her own father, enveloping her like a little girl.

That was the night I fell for her; there in my living room, with my father laughing and my babysitter snoring gently on the couch, Diana had danced me around and around until our breath heaved and the throw rug beneath our feet lay crumpled between us. She smelled like coffee and cinnamon and soap, bitterness mixed with an almost childish freshness that hasn't changed in the near fifteen years I've known her. Her hair was pinned back that night, wisps of brown slipping from her hair clips and tickling my feverish cheeks when she reached down to hug me goodbye.

"I think he likes you," my dad told her when he walked her toward the front door. My babysitter woke up as Diana left, and looked down at me, confused and groggy, as I sat smiling on the floor, pulling at a loose thread in the rug Diana and I had slid back and forth across the wood with our wild, dancing feet.

*

Diana's house now is still filled with memories of the life she shared with my father and me. My school pictures decorate the mantle above her fireplace, different versions of me smiling awkwardly out at her small living room; a wedding photo of her and my father stands on the piano in the corner, tucked behind a stack of her music books and tilted slightly toward the wall, as if incrementally she is removing it from its place in her home. She has a picture of me and Kim in the kitchen, a magnetic frame clinging to the refrigerator door above where she keeps her grocery list. She always asks about

Kim, in a voice so innocent and curious that I know she's never realized my feelings for her.

"I'm so glad you found a sweet girl," she'll tell me, even though she's only met Kim twice. Even though Kim is not really sweet.

"I think she's drunk," Kim told me the last time we saw Diana together. It was at a family friend's wedding, the night I watched Diana sway on the dance floor all alone, her shoes kicked off to the side, her eyes pressed shut, her lips parted and smiling.

"She's not drunk," I told Kim, watching the way Diana's stockinged feet slid across the marble floor, her hair hanging in loose waves, swinging in rhythm with the fabric of her dress. "She just loves to dance."

My father always used to talk about how Diana had the body of a dancer; she was still young when they met, her stomach flat and her breasts small and round. She wasn't beautiful, but she had the kind of tight, childless body that older women couldn't compete with, and her pale eyes smiled out from her freckled skin. Sometimes in restaurants or when we walked around the grocery store, my father would catch men looking at her and whisper, "I think he wants you to dance for him."

"I only dance for you," she'd say, and rock a bony hip up against my father. She had the kind of body that seemed to move slowly, languorously, as if she were constantly pushing her long limbs through a rough current of water.

*

When I was twelve I saw her naked. We were staying at a hotel in Myrtle Beach, in town for a cousin's wedding. My father got us two adjoining rooms, one for me and one for him and Diana, connected by a shared bathroom. I was excited to have my own space, with an enormous bed and a color television tucked into a heavy wooden armoire in the corner of the room. We spent an entire week there before the wedding, going to the beach everyday and ordering in room service.

"This is quite a life," Diana said one night, stretched out across the king-sized bed she and my father shared. We were in their room watching television, trays of half-eaten food surrounding us. Diana was wearing an oversized t-shirt with the neckline snipped out, so that the shirt slipped off of one shoulder revealing the yellow strap of her bikini. "We should just stay here forever."

My father smiled at her and ran a fingernail over her jutting collarbone. He slipped a finger under the strap of her bathing suit and lay back, his head resting on her sun-browned calf. "Your wish is my command." They laughed and she pressed a finger to his nose, smashing it down the way she always did when she thought he was being cute. He turned to me then, giving my arm a light squeeze. "Time for bed, kiddo," he told me, and began stacking up the room service trays.

I went back to my room and flipped on the television. It was late and all the sitcoms had ended, so I watched a talk show for a while. I started to fall asleep but pulled my eyes open every time I felt them drop shut; after a while I got up and wandered into the bathroom, a part of me knowing that I should leave my father and Diana alone. I remember pushing their bedroom door open from inside the bathroom, though I don't know what I planned to use as an excuse. I wonder now if I'd been trying to catch a glimpse of something I hadn't realized I wanted. I had always liked to watch Diana, enjoyed the feel of her delicate skin against my cheek when she kissed me goodnight, felt proud when she waited for me outside of school. But it wasn't until I eased open their bedroom door that I realized what it was I was looking for, what my half-sleeping body was edging me toward.

Diana and my father were lying silently on the bed, the light beside them still on and shining harshly down on their naked sleeping bodies. My father was pressed up against Diana, a bare leg thrown over her, her damp hair strewn out over his face. She was lying on her stomach, and from where I stood I could see how the brown of her thighs faded to a translucent white over the rise of her hips. It was as if someone had painted a bikini onto her naked body in stark white paint, sliding a brush over the smooth curves but somehow failing to conceal her. Her breasts were pressed flat against the mattress, and I could make out the blush of her nipple peeking out beneath the rise and fall of her narrow torso.

I don't know how long I stood there. I watched her breathe, felt the tumble of my own knocking heart, breathed in the clean, biting smell of her, stared at my father's thick arm wrapped around her body. I wanted to be him in that moment. I wanted to feel my own bare limbs tangled with hers, and I wanted the scent of her long sweaty hair in my face. I wanted the smell of her skin closer to me, next to me, pressing into my pores.

When her eyes opened, I didn't move. She seemed about to speak, and then thought better of it. I took a shaky step backward, back into the dark of the bathroom, and pulled the door quietly shut. I stared at the line of light that crept through the crack in the door, and after a moment it clicked off. I left the bathroom and climbed into bed, squeezing my eyes shut, committing every part of her to memory.

*

The next day was my cousin's wedding. He married a beautiful girl with big brown eyes and a ready smile. My father kept making jokes about how I had a crush on her.

"Where's your tongue, kid?" he asked me when I was introduced to her. "Acts like he's never seen a pretty girl before." He gave her a wink and pushed my hair off of my forehead with his broad hand. I shrugged and watched Diana. I liked going to events like this with her, events where we danced.

After the ceremony, there was a long reception and my father and cousin got drunk together. My father made toast after toast, then hooted and whistled as my cousin removed his new wife's garter belt. I stood beside Diana as my cousin swung the lacy belt around over his head, and when it sailed out over the crowds I reached up and caught it without thinking. Diana laughed and clapped as a group of people gathered around me.

"You have to put it on my maid of honor!" the bride yelled to me. She was tipsy and red-cheeked, and so was the girl that came toward me, giggling and shouting, tipping back a glass of champagne as she presented me with her raised leg. I looked over at my father, who was grinning and whooping wildly.

"Do it!" my cousin called out over the crowd of people. "Give her something to remember!"

The girl lifted her skirt, layers of lavender taffeta that scratched against my hand as I gripped her ankle. I could feel the sharp prick of new hair against the palm of my hand as I slid the belt up over her calf. She laughed and lifted her leg higher, passing her champagne off to someone and grasping my hand in hers. "Don't be shy!" she said, and the crowd grew louder.

I slid the garter up over her knee, my fingers catching in the folds of dimpled skin where her leg bent over my trembling hand. I caught Diana's eye, held her gaze as I had the night before, pictured the browns and whites of her peaceful, sleeping body. I imagined the smoothness of her thighs in the tangle of sheets, her small breasts pushed up against the bed. I inched the belt up further, my eyes on Diana, my hands on Diana, my fingers exploring the whites of her inner thighs, the stretches of skin where the sun hadn't reached.

"Whoa, there!" the maid of honor said to me then, laughing and pushing the belt back down around her knee. "I think we get the picture."

"That's my boy!" My father had come up behind us, put his arm around Diana's waist to watch.

Diana rolled her eyes. "You are wasted," she said to him, and put her hands on my shoulders. "So I think it's time for your son and I to have our dance."

She led me out onto the dance floor, the hem of her dress grazing my shoes as I followed closely behind her. She pulled me to her, smiling down at me the way she always did, holding my hand between her fingers the way she had the first night we danced. But this time we swayed together slowly, our bodies moving in wide circles around the floor, gentle and calculated, the dance no longer wild and thrashing as it had been the night we met. I pressed my other hand against the small of her back, feeling her bones tight against the fabric of her dress, fragile beneath my touch. Pressing my face to her neck, I could smell that familiar scent, that inexplicable bitterness blended with something powdery and youthful; dancing in her arms, our bodies clasped tightly together, she smelled at once like a child and a woman, and as she pulled me close to her like a son, I held onto her like a lover.

ASH WEDNESDAY

We're about to leave for church when my father calls and tells me to pack a bathing suit.

It's the middle of February, one of those warm winter days when flower buds get tricked into pushing up out of the ground and people get ahead of themselves, digging summer clothes out of trunks, wheeling dusty bikes out of garages. My mother is standing by the front door, studying her reflection in the hall mirror and pretending not to listen.

"You don't have to stay with him overnight," she'd told me the night before. "There's no reason to sleep on a couch just to save his feelings."

"I don't know where my bathing suit is," I tell him, nudging the kitchen door closed with my toe. I can see my mother point to her watch as the door swings shut. She's taking me and my brother to get our ashes before school, because our dad is picking us up in the afternoon to see his new apartment.

"You'll love this place, Emma," he'd said when he moved his stuff out of our house. "It's probably the only complex in Flatbush that's got a pool." I'd been standing in the doorway watching him lift boxes into the bed of his friend's pickup. As he passed by to get another armload, he tucked his fingers into the corners of my mouth and lifted my lips into a smile.

"Lighten up, kiddo."

My mother pokes her head into the kitchen. "Who is it?" she mouths, even though I can tell she knows it's him. She pulls at the collar of her shirt, which is stiff with starch and buttoned too high on her neck. She always looks uncomfortable in her church clothes, as if they've been tailored to another person's body.

I turn away from her and tell my dad I have to go. "We're going to get our ashes," I say into the phone. "I'll see you after school."

I hear the hiss of a lighter through the receiver. "Say hi to Jesus for me," he says, and I picture him blowing a thin blue line of smoke into his empty new apartment.

*

When my brother Brian and I were little, our mother would let us have food fights the night before Lent began. She'd make a huge bowl of instant pudding and stretch a plastic tablecloth over the dining table, and then we'd cover each other in chocolate and she wouldn't say a word. Sometimes our dad would join in, first acting angry about the mess and then suddenly plunging a fist into the bowl and slinging a handful of pudding across the table. Brian and I would take turns mashing the chocolate into his hair, spreading it across his cheeks and through his beard. He'd dab at the corner of his mouth primly and say, "Do I have a little something on my face?"

and we'd laugh wildly and overturn the bowl on his head and he'd just laugh along and let us. Once a neighbor had come by during our Mardi Gras ritual and he'd answered the door covered in chocolate. "Happy Lent!" he'd bellowed, offering no explanation, and I remember liking the idea of the neighbor going home and telling people about us, saying, "What a funny family they are." Most of the time we did everything the way normal people are supposed to do things.

When Brian told my parents that he was gay, that his friend Nick had actually been his boyfriend for over a year, my mother's first concern was with whether or not people already knew. "Do you think they hold hands in public?" she'd ask. "Have people figured it out?" She said this as if she might still be able to keep it a secret, as if maybe she'd found out in time to turn things around. I didn't bother telling her that everyone knew, that I'd known he was gay long before he ever had a boyfriend.

In church my mother would grip his hand tight and whisper along with the sermon, pulling him to her during the rite of peace with an urgent, "Peace be with you, sweetheart, peace, peace..." He'd catch my eye and mouth, "I think it's working," and I'd have to bow my head to keep our mother from seeing my laughter.

*

St. Barnabas is in Bay Ridge, a wide stone building set back from the sidewalk behind a high iron gate. When services aren't going on, the door is bolted shut, coils of chain braided through the fence. "To keep street people from sleeping on the seats," my mother explained, when

I said I thought churches were supposed to let in everyone. "To keep out people who are there for the wrong reasons."

Inside, the church transforms. The ceilings are high and the pews are built of red, glossy wood, the kneelers cushioned in dark velvet. The walls are lined in stained glass windows that stretch from the floor up into the eaves, and slices of sunlight push different colors into the church in the shape of intricate biblical scenes. The outside of the building betrays none of its interior grandness, as if the church is testing people's devotion, making sure they're willing to come inside without knowing what they might be in for.

We arrive a few minutes late and take our seats in the back balcony. We started sitting up there when Brian and I were little, because it was the only way our mother could keep us from whining our way through Mass. Getting to look out over the crowds had always made church infinitely more interesting, watching the shuffle of people below us as though we were guests of honor overseeing the proceedings.

My mother drops to her knees and begins reciting along with the congregation. She looks tired even beneath the soft shafts of stained-glass light, her skin pale except for two purple crescents beneath her eyes. She's leaning forward and gripping the pew in front of us, as if she's afraid she might miss something. "Holy God, we praise thy name, Lord of all, we bow before you." Her expression is solemn, almost scolding. My lips move along with hers. Sometimes I surprise myself with how easily my body remembers each prayer. "Infinite, thy vast domain, everlasting is thy reign."

Beneath my mother's curled fingers I see that someone has carved a word into the wooden seat back; I slide her hand to the side. *Love.* The carving looks messy, its edges rough and splintered, as if someone scraped it into the wood with the edge of a car key. My mother looks down at it, shakes her head. "Awful," she mutters, and spreads her palm out over the engraving. "Just awful."

"It could be worse," I whisper.

"Shh," she hisses. The congregation rises. "It's still graffiti." She begins singing along with the choir.

"No it's not, it's carved in." I start to sing too.

"It's disgusting."

Brian is standing on the other side of our mother, and he leans across her and whispers for us to be quiet. He likes to pretend that he takes this all very seriously. "Do you mind?" he'll say when I try to talk to him during Mass. "I happen to be accepting Jesus as my personal savior."

When I was twelve years old, my mother told me she was afraid that I might be a bad person. She'd said it matter-of-factly, as if it were something everyone already knew, a simple truth that she was finally surrendering to. "Sometimes I worry that you're just out of God's reach."

It was the middle of summer, a day when there was nothing to do but lay out in the backyard until our skin grew tight with heat and our legs itched from mosquito bites and the sharp stubble of freshly cut grass. Brian and I were on our stomachs, quizzing each other on state capitals, ripping weeds out from underneath us and poking them through openings in the chain-link fence. He was winning and it made me restless. "Let's do something else," I said, because I hated losing at things and Brian always won everything. I'd think up games and then he would win them, even if they were games I'd invented, games designed to defeat him.

"A mushroom walks into a bar," I began, and Brian turned to look at me, squinting and expressionless. "So the bartender says, 'Hey, we don't serve your kind here.'" I paused for effect.

Brian looked away, bored. "And so the mushroom goes—"

"But I'm such a fungi," he said, quiet and deadpan, like he couldn't believe he had such a moron for a sister. "You've told that one before, Emma." He rolled onto his back. "Washington."

I ignored him, tugging at a clump of weeds underneath me. My fingertips had turned a dirty shade of green; I rubbed them against the hot metal of the fence but it just seemed to push the color deeper into my skin. "I hate this game."

There was a car parked in the alley behind our house, a few feet from where we lay. It was for sale, had a big sign in the back window with a phone number scrawled across it. It was a huge station wagon, rusted blue with wooden panels along the doors, the kind of car with seats in the trunk that folded out so the passengers had to face backwards. I liked riding in cars like that, waving to the drivers behind me, making horrible faces and then diving down behind the heavy door when they started to look annoyed. "Let's buy that car."

Brian tossed a fistful of weeds at me. "Shut up."

"Let's call that number and make them think we want the car. They'll think they sold it and then we'll just never show up. It'll be funny."

"Washington," Brian said again.

I rolled away from him and sat up, lifting the hair away from my neck to cool off. "I don't know."

"Olympia. That was an easy one, Em."

"We could call and say something else. We could say they're under arrest."

"The police don't call to tell you you're under arrest, stupid."

"Then we'll think of something funny. Come on."

Inside, Brian insisted on being the one to talk. "At least let me call if we're doing this dumb idea," he said. "Besides, I sound older. They'll believe me." But a moment after he dialed the number, he panicked and thrust the receiver at me, slapping a hand across his mouth to stifle his laughter. "Do it," he hissed through his fingers. "Talk!"

I pressed my eyes shut and bit down on the insides of my cheeks to keep from giggling. I cleared my throat. "Hi, um..." I couldn't remember any of the things I'd thought of to say.

"Yes...?" the woman on the other end of the line asked.

"Hi, yeah, I was just calling to tell you..." I opened my eyes. Brian was watching me silently and I wanted to shock him. Impress him with my fearlessness. "I was calling to tell you there's been an accident." I grinned, watched for a change in his expression. His eyes searched me. "There was an accident on, um, on Lincoln Place, and your..." I paused. Brian looked suddenly solemn, almost afraid, as if in that moment he believed what I was saying and was scared of what might happen next. As if I had the power to determine the course of things. The line was silent, still, and I thought maybe the connection had been lost. That maybe the woman would be spared my cruelty. "Your husband died. He died in your station wagon."

I heard one shallow breath, a single choke of air. Then I slammed down the phone and saw my mother standing in the doorway, her expression horrified, heartbroken, as if some small sliver of her love for me had been carved irretrievably away.

*

When Brian and I meet in front of school at the end of the day, his ashes are gone.

"I wasn't going to walk around with dirt on my face all day," he tells me.

The cross on my forehead has faded to a smudge of gray, hardly more than a shadow across my skin. I'd stood in the girls' bathroom that morning and studied it, rubbed it with my fingers for a moment and then decided to leave it there. "There's nothing embarrassing about lenten ashes," my mother had said when she dropped us off in front of our high school that morning. "It's just like wearing a cross around your neck or keeping a rosary in your purse. It's something to be proud of."

"Yeah, I don't know why I kept mine," I say to Brian. "It's not like mom will know if we wiped them off."

I see my father making his way through a crowd of kids and he looks younger, messier somehow, as if the look of a free man is something you can slip on and wear around town. For a moment I watch him as a stranger and it seems odd that he's here, picking up his children from school; this version of my father looks like someone tied to nothing.

"We have to take the subway," he tells us as he approaches. "There's a goddamn boot on my car." He touches a hand to my forehead, like he's feeling for a fever. "Isn't it supposed to look like a cross?"

*

It's starting to get dark by the time we reach his building, but he tells us to get our bathing suits on anyway. "We'll jump the fence if we have to," he says, opening the door to his new apartment. "I'm getting my money's worth."

It's a small, dim studio and it smells like fresh paint and cigarettes. The floors are dusted with powdery chips of beige paint and open cartons line the walls. I see that one of them is marked *Kitchen Shit*, and I wonder how he and my mother ever ended up with each other.

"I didn't bring my bathing suit," I tell him, and drop my bag down on one of the boxes.

"Jesus, Emma, I called to remind you."

"It's February, Dad, everything's still packed away. I don't care about swimming anyway."

I've always hated swimming with my father. Even when Brian and I were little our dad was rough with us in the pool, as if he believed water made us sturdier somehow, more immune to getting hurt. When we'd dip in a hesitant toe, he'd yell, "Shit or get off the pot!" and push us in. Once I tried to learn how to flip off the side, went down to the end of our hotel's pool to practice on my own, and my dad followed. "You can't think about it so much," he'd said, as I stood there with my toes curled over the edge, staring into the blue, willing my body to flip. "It's just about doing it before you have time to get nervous." And then he'd lifted me up by my ankles and tossed me into the air, my head diving between my legs, my body slamming hard against the water. "Thatta girl," I'd heard him say when my head broke the surface.

He liked to hold Brian underwater. It was terrifying to watch even though it was supposed to be a game, and my father would laugh as if the whole thing were wildly amusing, while the shadow of Brian's body under the water thrashed and fought beneath his hands. I could always tell it scared Brian, that every time he came gasping up for air there was a part of him that had believed this time our father wasn't going to let him go.

"Don't!" our mom would shriek from the sidelines. "Don't, he hates it!" But Brian would never complain. He'd rise up out of the water bewildered, heaving, but he wouldn't say a word. The one time my father tried it with me, I screamed and cried and he never did it again. I remember being under the water, so near the surface that I could feel the summer air hot on the top of my head where my father's hands rested. I could hear him laughing the way he always did, the sound muted and distant, as if I were listening in from another room. When he finally let me up, I pounded my fists against him and he wrapped his thick fingers around my wrists, twisting until I was silent. My chest was tight and my eyes were blurred from the water, and for a moment I felt surprised that I'd been able to surface at all.

WRECKAGE

That the truth of it all could be reduced to a tidy square of text seemed impossible: her undoing nestled between other slender catastrophes, tabloid trash in the express line at the supermarket razing her life in ten words.

Theo was tucked into the front of the cart, sucking pear purée from a pouch they hadn't yet paid for; Alice was a sleeping bundle on her hip. She felt a reflexive urge to hand them over to someone in that moment—a police officer, a woman with children, the types of people they'd been instructed to look for in a crowd if they ever got lost.

Theo's dangling legs kicked at her stomach as she steered the cart out of line and toward the exit, a silent protest against this break from their routine, this pull in the thread of his ironed little life. She lifted him out and balanced him on her other hip as she headed for the parking lot, groceries abandoned, the baby food pouch clenched in his dimpled fist now a tiny first crime.

When they got home, she deposited a sleeping Alice into her toddler bed, lifting one socked foot to her lips for the last time. She left Theo in the kitchen with the housekeeper and said goodbye to him with a kiss on the head and the salve of a lie: *see you tomorrow, my guy.* But he wasn't hers, and tomorrow she would no longer exist within the taut radius of his three-year-old universe.

She left before anyone could tell her to leave, exiling herself before the world did it for her. She slipped an envelope of cash under her landlord's door to sever her month-to-month lease, left her supplies behind in Ben's studio like an offering, a meager atonement: slabs of cool, shapeless clay stacked high on the shelves, a mason jar packed tight with knives, the blank face of her sculpting wheel. The rumors had begun churning their way through social media, gathering dirt and grime along the way, and they'd surely landed in Ben's open hands by now. She imagined the facts of what she'd done flashing across his screen, coming to him in pieces, shrapnel slicing at him until eventually they hit bone. She couldn't bear the idea of seeing the naked hurt on his face, of hearing it in his voice over the phone, and so she'd sent him one line of text while sitting in traffic and then blocked his number. *I told you I'd fuck it all up.*

*

The rental was a few hours outside the city, shabby and uninviting, a husk of a place that might once have been charming. But that was what she wanted: to be somewhere no one would ever choose to be, where open days stretched blindly into weeks until she was forgotten. The house was available for as long as she needed it—a fact advertised like a gift but with the mildewed stench of desperation.

There was a narrow creek out back, and on her first afternoon she walked along the rocky seam where the dirt turned to mud, the water cold and rushing after a season of rain. The rocks were slimy with moss, slick and loose beneath her bare feet; she liked the feel of the ground shifting under her, a whole network invisibly arranging and rearranging itself. She dipped her fingertips into the water to feel the silky earth beneath her hands, and the mud was wet clay in her palms: amorphous, ready to be anything. She let it slide between her fingers and back into the cool water. What she needed was not yielding tenderness; what she needed was a hard fist of earth, something that would fight her back, that wouldn't grow soft and pliable in the warm cradle of her skin—she needed a writhing fever to churn her sickness to the surface.

She thought of Ben's studio back in the city—the vases she'd sculpted to line the sills of the windows, the animal figurines and piles of seashells and lone body parts that she'd carved from clay and then painted to look slick and organic: a bright red lump of heart, white stretches of bone, the alien coil of intestines. She wondered how long it would be before he threw them away, or if perhaps they were already gone. She wondered for a moment if maybe he'd broken them all, slammed them against the floor and walls, crunched the shattered pieces beneath his feet. But he wasn't that sort of person, more likely to wrap them carefully in newspaper and send them to one of her friends than allow himself the luxury of destruction.

*

She pushed her thumbs deep into the wet heft of clay, the sun hot on her bare back. Her phone had been buzzing relentlessly with unfamiliar numbers, and she watched the notifications pile up on the screen: two, three, four new voicemails, text messages in the double digits. She knew some of the messages had to be from Ben, and her cheeks flushed with shame at the idea of him realizing he'd been blocked, borrowing other people's phones to contact her. She stared at the red circle above the message icon, a blemish begging to be picked at, raw with the promise of pain and relief. But she couldn't stand the thought of hearing what he had to say, of absorbing his hurt without giving in to her own, and so she swiped the notifications away and returned to her work. She'd begun to use mud from the creek—left to bake in the sun, it hardened to a dusty pink and held its form—though most of what she made she tossed, a collection of unfinished creatures collecting in the yard like bones.

She often thought about the children while she worked, remembered their chubby hands plunging into tubs of play-doh, pinching the neon clay into approximations of living things. She pictured the orange-brown freckles dusted across Theo's nose, the bright honey of Alice's eyes, her pupils like perfect fossils encased in resin. She could still hear the sound of their little voices, all husky breath and grand pronouncements, profound and matter-of-fact in the way only children can be. She knew she didn't deserve to grieve any of it—not the children, not Ben or her job or her life—and the sickening guilt of what she'd done felt selfish, indulgent.

There was nowhere to put the pain that came with hurting people; all she could do was swallow it down and let the shards carve away at her from the inside.

She dipped her hands into the bowl of water at her side, then wrapped them around the slimy curve of clay that sat in front of her. She'd begun chiseling the delicate features of a woman into it, trimming away at the clay as if she were unearthing ancient bones, searching for a face buried beneath its surface. But she couldn't get the eyes right: they stared up at her like marbles, eerie and wrong, unblinking in their judgment. She grabbed her sculpting knife and began sawing at the top section of the woman's head, slicing along the bridge of her nose and cutting clean through. Then she removed the severed clay and smashed it between her fists, feeling immediately relieved, as if she'd averted a crisis, avoided shaping something malevolent into existence. She often thought about her art this way, secretly wondering if she could infuse good into the atmosphere by creating enough beauty, or if sculpting something grotesque meant living in a world that was just the slightest bit uglier, darker.

She pressed her knuckles into the bottom half of the woman's head, considered whether to hollow her out into a bowl, into a flower pot, into some other pleasing shape, some benign and practical vessel. She fussed with the woman's edges for a few minutes. She pressed shallow wrinkles into the bow of her lips to show that she'd lived a real life, smoothed out the contours of her cheekbones to suggest that the woman had once been beautiful. But she knew she was trying to push life into something lifeless, knead her palms against a heart that couldn't beat. She knew that when she was done this halved and emptied version of the woman would be discarded, another casualty added to the wreckage.

*

The tabloids had called it an affair, but the word had an unearned heft to it, a suggestion of intimacy that wasn't there; she didn't even have Andrew's number saved in her phone. The articles had left little to the imagination, published in the sorts of magazines that print first and asks questions later. Some of the details had been sleazy embellishments—there had been no private jet trysts, no salacious photos sent back and forth; she hadn't traded sex and discretion for the promise of future movie roles or gallery shows—but the seeds of the story, the parts from which the untruths grew, were all that really mattered.

The formless thing between them had in fact been ordinary and predictable, so clichéd that its doomed trajectory may as well have been mapped from the start. Andrew's pursuit of her had seemed both impossible and inevitable, the push of a bud from the tight bead of a leaf, the slow revolution of a plant toward the sun. Their mistakes splayed out in front of her the moment his fingers grazed the small of her back and lingered there like a question, and for half a year after that her life had been cleanly bisected. She'd spent her days playing pretend with his children, doling out snacks, giving baths and telling stories and singing lullabies. She'd aired silly grievances with the housekeeper and made polite chitchat with the children's mother. After work each day she'd gone to the studio to sculpt while Ben painted, ordered takeout and watched old episodes of *Curb Your Enthusiasm* curled into the warm hollow of his open arms. Her everyday life was quiet, subdued—contentment washed over her like the predictable comfort of their nightly reruns.

But then there were spaces of time layered between these things, hidden and malignant: afternoons spread out across a king-sized bed during naptime, or pressed into the tight air of the pantry as cartoons chattered in the other room, doing her job for her. Andrew became a habit she couldn't shake, like biting her nails to the quick even though it stung, even though the slender pleasure of whittling away at herself only left her feeling sore and ashamed.

She had no excuses for what she'd done, and she didn't bother blaming Andrew for any of it; disdain for his part in things seemed as pointless as hating a door that slams on your finger or a cement wall that dings your car. She'd made the same mistake over and over, piled her regrets like the bones of her half-formed creatures, hidden and discarded. She'd allowed her mind to slacken around the thought of all the suffering she might cause, all the lives she'd likely dismantle, until her guilt was shapeless, viscous. Then she'd say the things she knew she ought to say whenever she and Andrew were alone, when she'd hear the telling click of the door closing behind him: *wait, stop, this is wrong, we shouldn't, we shouldn't, we shouldn't.* And then she'd do it anyway, a silent resignation to something she wasn't sure she even wanted, like a dessert she ate simply because it was there. Because she kept mistaking emptiness for hunger.

THE ART OF NAVIGATING

We'd been on the road for less than an hour when my father pulled the car over and climbed out, shutting the door quietly and deliberately and walking off without a word, like he was finally through with us and this was goodbye.

My brother had been insisting we pull off the highway every few minutes, gasping and heaving and beating his little fists against the back of my father's seat, wailing that he was about to be sick, and then sitting back and announcing that it was a false alarm just as our car weaved through traffic and onto the shoulder. He'd tried putting his head between his legs, staring out at the horizon, squeezing his eyes shut and taking deep, heavy breaths; the only cure seemed to be my father negotiating through the Orange County traffic, cursing out the window at the honking cars as we pushed through to the side of the road. It wasn't until Kevin had assured us all that he was fully recovered and we had snaked our way back into the thick maze of cars that he leaned across me and threw up all over the center console.

We sat silently for a minute or so after our father got out of the car, watching his hunched, angry figure grow smaller in the distance, dust rising up off the road behind him. My mother was busy cleaning up Kevin's mess with a handful of papers from the glove compartment, and I wondered what sort of new fight would begin when my father decided to come back to the car. Even if the papers weren't important, I knew the sight of them crumpled in my mother's hands and coated in my brother's watery vomit would be enough to set him off.

Outside, the air was still and thick. We leaned against the car doors, swinging them open and closed, churning the heat around, trying to get the smell out of the seats. Kevin sat down on the ground, dust clouding up around him, his face pale and drained. "I wish we could just go home," he said, tracing a finger through the dirt that had settled on the tops of his sneakers. "What if I get sick again?"

"Then dad will put you out of your misery." I slammed the car door shut and sat down next to him. "He'll put us all out of our misery." I squinted, trying to see where our father was, but between the dust and the pools of heat swelling up from the pavement I couldn't see much of anything. I couldn't imagine how we were going to make it out of California at this rate, let alone halfway across the country. Even before Kevin had started feeling sick, the atmosphere in the car had felt tense, weighted with the pressure to have fun and act like a family. When I'd asked if we could turn on the radio, my father had answered with a barking and definitive "no" and I could see something in my mother's posture change immediately: a ripple of realization that made her sit up straighter, like her body registering that her expectations had been all wrong.

She'd packed up the trunk of our car tightly and meticulously, filling it with things she'd bought specifically for our trip, things we'd never owned before and would probably never use again: sleeping bags and kerosene lamps, hiking maps, tarps and ropes and windbreakers and flashlights. She'd filled plastic bags with bug spray and suntan lotion, folded our brand new outfits into neat little squares that fit into our brand new backpacks. She took pleasure in the preparation and anticipation, posting lists on the refrigerator door in the weeks leading up to our trip and marking things off with enthusiastic red checks, as though each item she tucked into the car brought us one step closer to taking the vacation that would change all our lives.

The plan was to go down the coast of California and then cut across New Mexico and Arizona and Texas, camping in the deserts and exploring the canyons and becoming the kind of family that spends day after day in the cramped space of cars and tents together without a second thought. My father had read books about how to survive in relative wilderness: the basics of hitching a tent and starting a fire, the art of navigating the desert with a compass and how to get a good night's sleep on earth that's frozen solid. I'd awaited our departure with a kind of detached anxiety, sure something would get in the way before the day we were scheduled to leave—a crucial business trip for my father, a fight between my parents, the collective realization that an adventure like this was not something any of us knew how to handle—until the day arrived when the car was packed and the route was mapped and the long, empty summer that lay ahead was snatched out from under me.

My mother came over and sat down beside us, crossing her legs beneath her and resting her head in her hands. She looked young to me sitting like that, a girl in distress on the side of the road, scratching at the bug bites on her arms and squinting against the sunlight with nothing to do but wait.

"I guess we're off to kind of a rough start." She stretched her bare legs out in front of her and pressed her sandaled feet against the dusty tires of the car. I could see the shimmer of blond hair coating her thighs, so pale you'd never know it was there if she weren't sitting still beneath the sun. "How are you feeling, bud?" she asked Kevin, and he took this as an invitation to fall heavily against her, digging his face into the crook of her armpit.

"Bad," he said, his voice muffled against her skin. "Very, very bad."

"I'm sure your dad will be back soon," she said, running her hands through his hair and pressing her chin to the crown of his head, and I could tell she wasn't sure at all. Our father had been gone nearly fifteen minutes, which is a long time when you've just left your family on the side of the highway. "I think he just needed some air." She looked over at me. "It's hard when he gets ideas in his head about how everything is supposed to go."

I nodded, even though I knew the same was true of her, maybe even more so. My mother was forever planning out the way she hoped things would be, waiting and hoping and planning and being let down, getting her heart broken over and over.

My father was gone for nearly an hour, and when he finally returned he was somber and unapologetic, handing off the keys to my mother and climbing into the passenger's seat without a word. I was surprised when my mother reached for the map and pulled back onto the highway to head southward. I had assumed that this would be enough to guide us back in the direction of home, that by dinnertime we'd be back in our house, pretending the day's events had never happened. But instead we continued on our way in the direction my parents had plotted out, our car following the thick red line my mother had traced along the California coast of the map. The sun had begun to sink below the line of trees and I wondered where we were going to spend the night, how we were going to put up a tent in the darkness of some unknown campsite and what we were going to eat for dinner, but I felt glad for the calm silence of the car.

The sun had nearly set when I felt the car lurch forward and slide sideways. The tires screamed against the road and our suitcases thumped around loudly, toppling down over the seat behind me and into our laps.

"What in the hell!" my father bellowed, sitting upright as we came to a stop. I could see my mother's hands trembling as she gripped the wheel. We were the only ones out on the road but there were houses on either side and signs for food and motels in the distance. The empty stretch of highway in front of us was fading to purple beneath the dark sky. "What the hell just happened?"

"I hit something," my mother said, her voice shaky. "Didn't you feel it? It ran out in front of us. I tried to avoid it but I hit it."

"For Christ's sake," my father said, unbuckling his seat belt. "Is that all? You nearly killed us over some goddamn rodent?" He shook his head and reached for the door. "Get out, I'll drive. Scared the crap out of me for roadkill."

"I think it was a cat," my mother said, and I could see tears streaming down her face. "We're in a neighborhood, it's someone's cat. It isn't roadkill."

But my father was already out of the car, coming around to the driver's side, his hands balled into tight fists. He didn't look under the car to inspect whatever it was we'd hit, just yanked open the door and told my mother to get out. When she climbed out, I did too.

"Get back in the car, Katie," he said, but I followed my mother around to the front of the car, afraid of what we'd find, my heart beating fast from the shock of the impact and from the prospect of what we may have hit.

Beneath the front tires, just under the bumper, I saw the cat, sprawled and motionless, and for a moment it seemed as though he were dozing in the sun or waiting for someone to come by and scratch his belly. I leaned in closer and I knew that he was dead. He lay split open, and I heard the sharp intake of my mother's breath and then she put her hand up to my face and said, sad and quiet, "Don't look, sweetheart," as though this were something she could save me from. I moved away from her and stood, looking. His eyes were still partly open, just wide enough for me to see a slice of electric yellow, and the fur above them was caked with brown-red blood. He looked alive to me, like he'd been frozen mid-movement and could reanimate at any moment, lift gracefully off the ground to shake out his fur and lick his wounds until they sealed back up. I wanted to reach out and touch him, to pet the small stretch of his flank that remained perfect and whole, to feel the rise of bones as they fused back together beneath my fingers.

A HISTORY OF EXISTING LIFE

The first time I saw my father after nearly four years, he threw a plate of eggs at me and accused me of having an affair.

"Cheating bitch," he'd shouted, and the plate had smashed against the wall behind me. I could feel the spatter of yolk on my arm as he pulled the blankets up over his bare white legs and grabbed a bottle of syrup from the tray in front of him. "Crazy French *cunt*." He hurled the bottle at me and it broke open at my feet.

He was propped up in bed—*bedridden*, Nathan had warned me when I said I was coming to visit—and his body looked frail, sunken, like the body of an old man. His graying skin hung in folds around his eyes, as if the bones of his face were shrinking away. He glared at me, squinting. "How long have you been making a fool of me?" he asked. He swept the tray from his lap and it clattered to the floor. "How long has this been going on?"

I brushed bits of egg from my shirt. "Daddy..."

"Get the hell out of my house."

I felt a hand on my arm. Nathan pulled me out into the hallway, shutting the door behind us. I slid to the floor. The egg yolk had begun to dry against my skin, and

Nathan ran a dishtowel down my arm and the yolk lifted off in flakes, like the skin of a snake.

*

When I was growing up, my father refused to ever make a scene in public—he was a different person when we were out of the house. I found my public father fascinating, a stranger that I'd watch in awe. In public he smiled a lot; he made jokes and laughed loudly; he kept a protective hand against the small of my mother's back, and sometimes I'd feel the soft weight of his palm on the crown of my head, as if he were saying to the world: *These belong to me.*

Before we went out, my mother would smooth back my hair with bright satin ribbons, scrub my and Nathan's fingernails until our skin was raw and our nails were as smooth and pink as seashells. She'd put on a dress that swished and rustled as she walked, and my father would look at her as though the two of them shared some wonderful secret. The world outside our house made him into a content man, and being beyond those confines made my mother different too. Around other people she was charming, alive. It seemed like she touched my father more, as if being seen as his wife reminded her that that's what she was. That he was hers and that wives touched their husbands. At home she left him alone. Even as a child I could see how fiercely she loved him, but it was a hesitant love. It was the love of someone trying not to squeeze too hard, afraid that handling the object she cared about most meant that surely it would break.

As much as I liked this public version of us, there was something about knowing my father would always keep his cool that made me fight against him, simply because it was the only time I could. I was overcome by a need to test him, to see how far I could get. I was a doctor prodding at my patient, laying pressure on different spots, pushing against sensitive organs to see what would finally make him cry out. It was exhilarating, seeing my father fail to react.

Sometimes I'd play tricks on him, watch the flush of red that crawled up his neck and into his cheeks, threatening a thunderous anger that would never erupt when we were in the safety of the outside. Once at a fancy restaurant I'd unscrewed the lid of the salt shaker under the table and then placed it casually beside him, waited for him to shake it out over his steak, tried to hold in my laughter when he'd emptied the entire contents onto his plate in one dramatic mound of white. He'd hissed something at my mother under his breath, his hand shooting into the air to alert the waiter, but that was all he could do. He never asked me if I'd opened the lid. He never yelled. My mother ordered him another steak and he stayed silent and still, his eyes fixed on something beyond our table. She pretended nothing had happened.

My mother never had it in her to discipline us. She said that she'd been taught everything the wrong way and didn't want to make the same mistakes with us. "Yelling and hitting doesn't solve anything," she'd said to me once. "It doesn't teach anything but how to yell and hit."

The only time my mother scared me was when she spoke German. She hardly ever did—that was a part of herself she'd sealed off, leaving Germany at sixteen and shedding her accent almost entirely—but when she did speak it, the language transformed her. She spoke loudly and quickly, her voice somehow more resonant. In English her voice was soft, childlike, and when she raised it the result was almost comical. But speaking German, she seemed to me someone else entirely, someone commanding and sturdy. I wondered if my German mother was one who would demand obedience if only I could understand her. On Sunday afternoons she'd sit at the kitchen table and talk to her sister, and her conversations would fill the house with words that were a mystery to the rest of us. Sometimes on those days I would see her catch my father's attention. A look would pass across his face when he watched her that I rarely saw unless he was listening to a news story on the radio, or reading contracts for work. It wasn't a smile, but an expression of absolute concentration. Not amazement, or even admiration; just focus. I imagined that if he were in a movie, that would be the moment when he would stand glassy-eyed, mouth agape, while someone humorously waved a hand in his face and he looked on, oblivious.

*

I was fourteen when I met my father's mistress. It was a Fourth of July party, the week after my birthday. Nathan was away at camp in Monterey and my mother said I could stay downstairs until midnight if I promised not to drink and not to brag to Nathan about the party when he got home. I wore a bikini top I'd found in my mother's closet, lavender triangles that hung loosely over my breasts and tied together with beaded string that dug hard into my skin. My mother laughed when she saw me but said the color made me look tan so I left it on, wore it down to the party with a pair of tight denim shorts and a gold locket I'd gotten for my birthday.

Margaux was sitting on a piano bench next to my father, who was playing along to a jazz record and singing under his breath, his voice gravelly, slurred with liquor. She was smiling and swaying, a cigarette pinched between her lips, her dress draped low on her shoulders so I could see the hard angles of her collarbones. She was tall and pale, with powdery skin and a thick twist of black hair pinned to the back of her neck. Her arms were thin and she had no breasts at all, her chest nearly concave beneath the sheer fabric.

"Bonsoir, Caroline," she said, but she pronounced it "Caro-leen," and her throat caught on the sounds as if she were trying them out for the first time.

"Why are you dressed like that?" my father asked when he saw me. He lifted his fingers from the piano and slammed down the cover. "For Christ's sake, Caroline."

Margaux smiled up at me, wrapped an arm around my waist, her long fingers stretching around the curve of my hip. She held an ashtray in her hand and the glass was cold against my skin. "I think she looks lovely," Margaux said, and her accent made each word sound new.

I smiled back, pulled my stomach in tight. Her eyes were level with my torso and I wanted her to notice the cinch of my waist, the new rise of my breasts.

My father's eyes flicked across my bare body and he shook his head. "You look like a hooker," he told me.

"Let her have her fun," Margaux said. She swirled the wine in her glass, lifted the glass to her lips. "While her body is young and exquisite." She smelled like ginger and cigarettes.

When I found her and my father in the den a few hours later, I didn't recognize her for a moment. My father was holding her long black hair in his fists while she leaned naked over a gold-plated mirror, her face pressed close to the tidy rows of powder. She looked up at me and just smiled. My father was bare-chested behind her, his legs wrapped around her frail white frame; he had the heels of his feet tucked between her thighs.

"Get out, Caroline," he said, but I barely registered the sound of his voice. Margaux was silent. Her breasts hung small and limp over the hollow of her stomach.

And then my mother was there, pulling me from the room, shutting the door noiselessly behind us. "It's past midnight," she said. Her eyes were dark, the blues and grays of her makeup smudged across her lids like the spread of fading bruises. She looked down at my bathing suit; the fabric sagged around me and I felt suddenly childish. She shook her head, tugged at the strings behind my neck. "You stubborn thing, you wore it all night long."

*

Downstairs, Nathan told me that music was the only thing my father always seemed to remember.

"Half the time he doesn't know who the hell I am, but the man could pick Charlie Parker out of a lineup." He poured me a cup of coffee and slid a bowl of sugar across the kitchen table. Above us, the sound of my father's record player pulsed through the floorboards. "Once he wakes up a little more he'll be glad you're here, even if he's not sure who you are." Nathan stood at the kitchen window, his arms folded tightly across his chest, his foot tapping along to the shrill whine of saxophones. I wondered for a moment how he could stand living alone in this enormous house with a man who couldn't even remember his name.

"He called me a cunt." I poured some milk into my coffee mug and it sloshed over the edge. Nathan reached across me and smeared the spill away with the palm of his hand, and I smiled over at him. "Two strokes and he still knows I'm the bad one."

Nathan laughed and wiped his hand along his pants. "I'm sure that wasn't meant for you, Caroline."

My father was a month shy of his seventieth birthday and dying of liver disease, having suffered nearly enough brain damage to wipe his memory clean. "He's only got a little while left," Nathan had told me when he called to let me know he was moving to Montauk to be with our father. "A few months at the most. You should come."

My father lived in what used to be my parents' vacation house, a huge bungalow on the tip of Long Island that he and Margaux moved into when I was eighteen, a few years after he divorced my mother. The house sat right on the beach, its entire back wall built of glass so that the blond wood of the ceilings and floors framed the stretch of beach outside like a mural. When it stormed the ocean rolled up over the dunes, feet from the house, and when I was younger I imagined the waves lifting the house from its roots like a tooth pulled from its gums, carrying us off into the Sound while we slept.

"Has he mentioned Mom at all?" I stirred my coffee around, lifted a sip into the bowl of my spoon.

"Not really. He talks about women all the time but I never know who he's talking about. He's always saying he has parties to go to." Nathan shrugged and sat down beside me. "I guess they're parties that happened twenty years ago."

When I told my mother that my father was dying, she said it was because men can't survive without women. "Women can outlive their husbands by fifty years. They can live alone their whole lives," she told me. "But men without women just fade away."

My father left us on a Tuesday. There was no lead-up to his departure, no screaming or fighting. He didn't sleep on the couch in the days before it happened, or sit us down for a serious discussion. One morning he said simply, "Your mother and I are getting a divorce," and he had a suitcase in his hand when he said it. Then he kissed me on the top of my head, gave Nathan's shoulder a squeeze, and left the house like it was any other day. As if he'd just told us that he'd decided to sell the car or buy a new set of golf clubs. As if he were only mentioning it out of courtesy, and it had nothing to do with us at all.

In the weeks after he left, his absence seemed to register with my mother in pieces. After a few days she remembered not to take down four plates at dinnertime, and a week later I found my father's bottle of scotch in the trashcan, still half-full. The life disappeared from her face gradually, imperceptibly at first, like the sky slowly emptying itself of the moon. She'd sit by the window that looked out over our backyard, a book open in front of her, and stare. Sometimes she'd flip a page, as if suddenly remembering there was something she was supposed to be doing, but I don't think she ever read. For the first time that I could remember, my mother seemed messy and unglued. Deep purple crescents formed beneath her eyes; her hair was greasy, knotted on top of her head and pinned haphazardly in place. Dust collected in corners and along the edges of the walls; piles of laundry overflowed from wicker baskets. Sometimes she'd walk slowly around the house looking at things, gripping cups of tea that she never seemed to drink, fixing her attention on a vase of flowers or a book on the bookshelf so intently that I wondered if she was seeing something no one else could. I'd find full mugs of tea all around the house, the teabags inside heavy and plump with sitting water, and it was strange not to see the waxy red stamp of her lipstick on their rims. I'd only seen my mother without lipstick a handful of times in my life.

By the time my father came to pick up the rest of his things and it was clear he wasn't coming back, my mother was nothing more than a shell of herself. She didn't even look at him. I thought I'd be proud of her for that. I thought I didn't want him to have the satisfaction of seeing what he'd done to her, and in the days before he came over for the last time, I spent every moment on edge, terrified that my mother would break down at the sight of him. But instead she kept her back to the living room, her bare feet propped up on the windowsill, a book balancing on her knee. She had one hand pressed over her mouth, as if she were afraid that if she let go something might escape. She was silent and motionless, but I didn't feel relieved at all. I felt like he was getting away with everything.

On his way out of the house, my father put down the crate of clothing he was carrying and looked down at me, his face solemn. He cupped his palm under my chin with a tenderness I wasn't used to, and reflexively I jerked away from him. Something in his eyes changed immediately; a look flashed across his face that was familiar to me in a way that the gentle feel of his skin on mine was not. He reached down and lifted the crate. "And we have a saltwater pool," he said, heading toward the door, as if he were continuing a conversation we'd already been having. His voice sounded formal, business-like. "It's much nicer than the one you've got here. Bigger."

"Okay," I said, because there was nothing else to say. The idea of visiting him in his new house seemed unimaginable: his books lined up on someone else's shelves, our paintings displayed on foreign walls, seemed like organs transplanted into the body of a stranger.

*

When Margaux died last year, my mother said I should go to the funeral. I was living in Los Angeles, a few miles from my childhood home where my mother still lived, and I refused. I didn't want to see my father destroyed by the loss of a woman, when leaving my mother hadn't hurt him at all.

He married Margaux on Christmas day, on our beach in Montauk. It was below freezing that day, and the sand was coated in a thick layer of snow, but Margaux wore a sleeveless white dress that made her nearly indistinguishable against the heavy gray sky. The white of her arms and shoulders blurred with the snow and her black hair, hanging loose, looked like a mistake, a smudge of ink across a blank page.

I loved when it snowed in Montauk; the image of snow against beach was like one photograph superimposed on another. It reminded me of a picture my father had bought for my mother's birthday the year before they divorced, a picture he told us was titled "A History of Existing Life". It was a series of photographs developed as one: an enormous volcano sprouting up from a wet city sidewalk, reaching up into the sky, erupting into a lush landscape of wildlife swallowed by a violent waterfall spilling down the volcano's sides. At the base of it all, a couple kissed beneath an umbrella, their eyes pressed shut, their arms clasped around each other, the waterfall inches from their bodies, about to sweep them away.

"The incongruity of existence," my father explained when he brought it home to my mother, "is what makes this piece beautiful. Water erupting from fire, life in the ruins, a love story amidst destruction." He pointed to the couple. "They're facing death and they don't even know it. They're totally oblivious."

My mother studied the picture and then shook her head. "No, they know they're going to die," she said. She almost never disagreed with him. She ran a finger along the glass of the frame, leaving a tiny smudge over the arc of the couple's umbrella. "That's the point. The one thing that never changes is that humans live their whole lives with that horrible knowledge. Knowing their existence will end and they'll lose everything. Every single beautiful thing." She shrugged, moving closer to the photograph, as if to study each of its contours. "It's all so fleeting, and we do all it anyway." Then she looked over at my father, her eyes defeated. "We know the end is coming, but all we can do is hold on."

*

After Nathan and I had dinner together, Nathan went up to our father's room to help him out of bed and downstairs into his wheelchair. "It's what he does every night," Nathan had explained as he piled our dishes into the kitchen sink. "He just wheels around the house and talks. It's the only time he doesn't act like he's dying."

I could hear them upstairs together, my brother's voice low and even, my father's rising shrilly over the creaks of his bed like the protests of a child. I heard their footsteps reach the top of the stairs and start to descend, the clap of their feet slow and deliberate. I turned on the kitchen faucet and watched our dinner plates fill with water, the remains of our food swirling down the drain.

I could hear him in the living room, settling into his wheelchair, the rubber of the wheels squeaking along the wood floors. Nathan came into the kitchen and told me he was going to rest upstairs, that I should wake him up when Dad was ready to go up to bed.

"Don't leave me alone with him," I whispered, but Nathan just shook his head and started toward the staircase.

"He's still the same person, Caroline," he told me. He smiled. "If that's any consolation."

I was still washing dishes when my father rolled into the kitchen. He stopped in the doorway, watching me silently.

"Hi, Daddy." I leaned back against the counter, waiting for him to speak. I took a sip of wine. My father just studied the blanket that was draped across his lap, twisting it between his fingers. He smiled down at the fistful of fabric, then up at me. "I don't know why you're always trying to make me wear flashy shirts," he said and wheeled further into the room. His eyes were unfocused and a light, diluted blue. I didn't say anything. His long, slender hands were pale and pockmarked, the skin stretched out over his bones so thinly that I could see each vein snaking around the rise of his knuckles. His fingernails were chipped and yellowing, and they snagged on the loose threads of blanket. He held the blanket up for me to see. "These are the kind of shirts I like, Margaux," he said, his voice quiet. "Not too flashy, not too casual. Just right."

"Daddy." I crossed over to him and put my hand on his. It felt natural even though I hadn't touched him in years. His hand was cold and damp beneath mine. He looked at the wine glass in my hand, shook his head.

"I thought we had a deal," he said, wrapping his fingers around the glass's stem. "Nothing to drink this week."

"It's me, Dad." I pried his fingers from my glass and stepped back. His eyes searched me, accusing. "Daddy. It's Caroline."

"I've been true to my word since Saturday. Not a brandy, not even a cigarette." His gaze was fixed on the floor. "Benny offered me a line and I said no siree."

I went back over to the sink, looked out the kitchen window into the darkness. I could hear the low rumble of waves smacking against the shore outside, but all I could see was black. "Do you feel okay?" I asked.

I heard my father sigh behind me. "How do you think I feel? I'm about to die." He cleared his throat and it turned into a loose, rattling cough. I turned back to him and he was wheeling toward me. "You're probably counting the days." He reached up and snatched the wine glass from my hand. He rolled it between his palms, his eyes set on mine, and then smashed it on the floor. "I told you not to *drink*." He wheeled across the shards of glass and they crunched beneath his weight. "No wonder you died first."

*

Nathan was already asleep when I heard my father calling out for him from his bedroom. I was lying awake in my old room, on the canopy bed my parents bought me on our first trip to Montauk. The room smelled like vacation, like unused bedsheets and cold beach air. I closed my eyes and tried not to listen to my father's voice through the walls.

"Nathan," he called, and I wondered if that would make Nathan happy—if waking to the sound of our father remembering him would make his place here seem somehow more worthwhile. We were the first ones to fade from our father's memory, and sometimes I wondered if Nathan resented him for it.

"Nathan," my father called out again, and then quieter, "Caroline."

The sound of my name through the wall slammed against me, knocked my heart into a quick, nervous beat. "I'm coming, Daddy," I called.

My father was sitting up in bed and the lamp beside him was on, spilling light onto his face so that the deep creases around his lips and eyes caught in the shadows, making him look old, used up. His hands hung limp at his sides, palms up, defeated, as if to say, *I simply don't know.*

"Are you okay?" I asked, and he shook his head slowly, looking up at me.

"She wasn't even dead," he said, pushing away his blankets. He was wearing a pair of pajama bottoms with candy canes on them, red and green fabric with flecks of cartoon snow swirling down the legs. He looked like a little boy. "Your mother wasn't even dead when they buried her."

I crossed over to his bed. "Mom is alive, Daddy. Mom didn't die." I smoothed the blankets back around him, covered his legs.

"Caroline," he said, louder, deliberate. "I saw her move at the funeral. I told someone but they ignored me. Her hands were trembling. I told her to open her eyes but she couldn't. She was so weak." He rubbed his hands together, pressed them to his face. "I've never seen her so weak as she was at that fucking funeral."

"Daddy," I said. I sat down on the edge of the bed beside him. "Do you mean Margaux?"

He lifted his hands from his face and looked at me, confused. "Of course I mean Margaux. She was so brave that day." I saw something change in his eyes, a flicker of memory. He looked straight at me. "Your mother was never brave like that." He placed his hand on mine and leaned back against the headboard. "Margaux loved me less than I loved her," he said, and his eyes were closed. "I loved her so much and she cheated on me all the time. Did you know that, sweetheart?" His hands were rough against mine, dry and calloused, and he rubbed his thumb up and down my forearm as if he were trying to soothe me. "She said I was the only lover that she *loved*. She said that made all the difference." He laughed. "Boy was she something."

I reached for the lamp switch. "It's late, Daddy."

"We had a lovely life together, though. Whether she loved me or not, it was damn lovely."

*

My mother still wore her wedding ring sometimes, long after my father left her. She never remarried, never went on dates or had men over to the house. We'd go shopping together and I'd wonder why she bothered, why every morning she lined her lips in red lipstick and wore expensive clothes, why she got a facial each month, who she bought silky slips and lace stockings for. I hated when she bought new dresses, pictured her alone in her closet snipping off the tags and hanging the dresses behind rows of clothes, realizing she had nowhere to wear them. Sometimes I'd see her twirl her wedding ring frantically around her finger, lift it up toward the knuckle and then drop it down again, the habit of a woman married twenty years. She'd look down at it and I'd wonder how the feel of it on her skin didn't destroy her, how the thought of my father didn't make her hurl it against the walls. I asked her once how she could still love him.

She slid the ring up over the slope of her knuckle then back into place, said simply, "Because I do."

The light wisps of my mother's hair had begun showing the first glimmers of gray, silvery against pale blond. She'd tried dyeing them but they just resurfaced, like wrinkles creasing their way through layers of thick, creamy makeup. Still, she looked young and beautiful to me.

"It's easier to be left," she'd said. "It's out of your hands. What's impossible is choosing to lose what you love. So I stayed until he wasn't there anymore."

*

My father fell asleep with his hands still clasped around mine, and I stretched out next to him, listening to the rumble of his shallow breathing. His heartbeat was slow, uneven, and part of me expected it to taper off, to grow lighter and lighter like retreating footsteps until it rested silent in his chest. But it kept going, vibrating against me.

I fell asleep next to him, and in the middle of the night we awoke at the same time. He looked at me, his eyes bright and blue and clear, the eyes of someone young. He gripped my hand in his, held on tight until my fingers were nearly numb. I knew that the memory of me had died away again. He watched me and I stayed very still, my eyes never breaking from his, until something in his face changed and he looked relieved, calmed, as if he just had to be sure that anyone had been there at all.

THE AUTHOR

Shelagh Powers Johnson received her MFA in Fiction from American University and is currently working on her PhD in English. She teaches Literature and Creative Writing at Bowie State University, where she also serves as faculty editor of the university's literary magazine, *The Torch*. Her work has appeared in *The Portland Review, The Plentitudes, Ghost Parachute and The Grace and Gravity Anthologies,* among others, and her writing has been nominated for Best Microfiction and Best Small Fictions. You can view her TEDxTalk, "Creative Writing: A Transformational Practice," on YouTube and find her at www.shelaghjohnson.com.

9 781965 412039